I0555920

Vampire's Lair

Children of the Wild, Volume 3

Prudence MacLeod

Published by Prudence MacLeod, 2024.

VAMPIRE'S LAIR

First edition. February 20, 2024.

Copyright © 2024 Prudence MacLeod.

ISBN: 978-1927478639

Written by Prudence MacLeod.

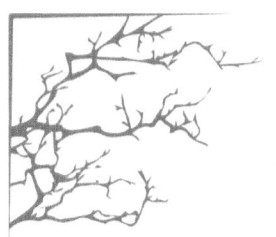

Vampire's Lair

Third Book in the Children of the Wild Series
by

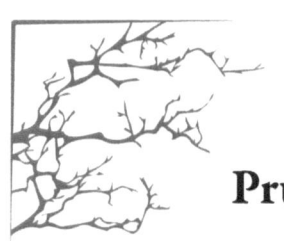

Prudence MacLeod

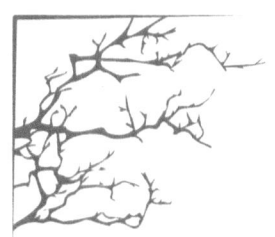

Blood Trail

Blood slowly dripped from the blade of the axe held tightly in her hand. Although the drops made no sound as they hit the mossy forest floor, she was keenly aware of each and every drop slipping away, watching its painfully slow descent to the ground. Each drop that fell held her transfixed as if it was the only thing in her world.

A flicking tongue licked hungry lips as another droplet fell towards the moss as though in slow motion. She fought for control, to break the maddening focus brought on by the searing need for blood. "Control, must regain control. Hungry, so hungry, burning thirst ..."

A soft voice cut through the fog in her brain. "What's your name? Think, girl, what's your name, tell me." It wasn't actually a voice, just a memory of a voice heard ages ago, but it was enough.

"Marlene," she gasped, "my name is Marlene." That did it. The rest of the world snapped back into focus.

The baying of the dog and the shouts of the men were clear to her now. Gripping the axe tightly, she ducked behind a large tree and fought the distracting scent of blood. "The damned bear can wait," she muttered, as she allowed her body to change into the vampire's killing mode. "I need to feed."

The hound was the first to reach the clearing and find the bodies of the two men. He snuffed about for a moment, then threw back his head and gave a long howl. As he lowered his head he made eye contact with the vampire. Instantly dropping to a submissive posture, he began to crawl away.

That's when the men arrived, swearing as they ran. Suddenly spotting the bodies they skidded to a halt. "Aw Jesus, it's Jimmy, I told

3

him to wait for me. Now I gotta tell his Ma what happened to him. Go on dog, find me that damned bear. Go on, git movin.'"

The hound just whimpered and slunk farther away from the angry man. "What the hell is the matter with you? You've seen dead men before. Get after that damned bear." Still the dog didn't move. "Fine, if you won't hunt, then I've got no reason to feed you."

With a snarl on his face he leveled the shotgun at the cowering dog, but the beast was looking past him. An axe flew through the air to shatter the skull of his companion. Before he could pull the trigger he was struck from behind, and needle sharp fangs bit deeply into his neck. As he struggled helplessly in the vampire's grip, the dog fled.

Nearly mad with the blood thirst and the killing lust, Marlene forced herself to wait. That shotgun could be a problem for one so newly risen. When the man turned away to threaten the dog she hurled the axe then charged.

The force of her body slamming into him would have sent the man flying had she not gripped him tightly. Before he could utter a startled squawk her fangs bit deep, puncturing the main artery in his neck. Hot blood spurted into her greedy mouth, and she moaned with delight as she drank noisily.

The shotgun fell from feeble hands as he struggled weakly against the vampire's steely grip. The struggles lessened then stopped, but she continued to drink greedily, the blood coursing through her like the fires of life, returning her strength, her memories, and her power over them all. Still craving more, she thrust him away.

"Control, Marlene, get control of it." She was licking her lips, and her burning gaze held him transfixed. "Are there more of you?"

He tried to crawl farther away from her, but her sudden movement stopped him. She grabbed the front of his shirt and held him off his feet in the air. "*Are there more of you? More hunters?*"

That terrible voice from a distant hell demanded a response, a response he could not refuse. "No," he whimpered, "just us four."

She hurled him away then and shook herself to gain control of the killing lust. So strong. The blood thirst was so strong when first arisen, but she had to get control of it. Oddly, it was the dog's terror that did it for her. She'd always loved dogs, and her compassion for the poor beast broke through the lust for blood.

The hunter was trying to crawl away, but she turned with liquid grace and hauled him to his feet. She dragged him back beside the bodies of the three men who'd been killed with the axe. Placing the axe in his hands, she spoke in that voice from a distant hell. "*Hold this, hold it tightly. Take this axe to the police, tell them you killed these men. You fought over a woman. You're sick in your soul at what you've done and want to confess. You will never speak of me to anyone, ever. Obey me. Go!*"

Stumbling and weak from loss of blood, the man staggered away, back the way he'd come. As soon as he was out of sight Marlene allowed herself to return to human form. She gazed down at the gaping blood stained hole in her shirt created when she'd taken a shotgun blast to the chest. With a sigh she removed the ruined shirt, bra, and jacket. She'd have to bury them.

For a moment she lightly traced her freshly healed chest with long delicate fingers. Not even a scar. Her breasts gleamed in the sun as she set out along the trail. "Now to find that damned bear."

Darkness was falling when she stopped. Normally she would have continued. She could see quite well in the dark and preferred to hunt at night, but she was still weak and needed more blood. Feeding from the human had restored her faculties and her form, but not her great vitality. For that she needed more blood, but not necessarily human.

The deer had no chance as she slammed into it, knocking it to the ground. It struggled weakly for a moment then lay still. The vampire drank greedily until there was no more to be had.

Marlene sat back and licked her lips, her blood lust satiated at last, her great strength and vitality returning. She hurled the carcass off the trail and set out again. A short while later she found a likely spot for the night.

"Tomorrow I need to steal a shirt somewhere," she muttered, as she settled down beneath a tree. This wasn't the first time she'd slept out in the forest, but it wasn't on the top ten list of her favorite things to do. With a deep sigh she drifted off to the land of dreams.

Marlene awakened at daybreak. Normally she'd have tracked the bear by scent through the night, but so soon after the resurrection she'd needed the rest. Now the sun was bright, and her dark sunglasses had been smashed in the clash with the hunters. She moved deeper into the shade of the trees to wait for nightfall.

This was taking far too long, the king would be angry, and she missed her beautiful apartment in Paris. Hell, she missed the small farm she'd grown up on. This living in a place that was little more than a dormitory was annoying. Marlene was losing her love of New York living. She longed to return to her estate in France.

"Damn that murdering bear anyway." Marlene decided to blame the bear. She'd been all packed for her vacation to Paris when she got the word. The queen had a vision of a killing, the king suspected a were-bear, and there was no one else available to send. She'd been sulking as she reached the area, not paying close attention, and had been surprised by the hunters.

They'd jumped her looking for an easy rape, but a man with an axe had interfered before she could deal with them. Marlene had taken the full blast of the shotgun and revived to find herself alone with two dead bodies. With any luck she had covered that issue upon her revival.

"So, who the hell is the guy with the axe, where did he go? Why did he interfere? And, more importantly, why had he been naked, and where the hell did the bear go?"

Marlene continued to mutter as the day wore on. In truth she was just fussing to get her mind off the blood lust. She knew she still needed more human blood to fully restore her human appearance as well as all her memories. The deer had returned her strength, but she could still feel traces of the cat's whiskers on her face. The vampire was not happy.

She set out again near dusk. The scent of the bear was mixed with the man now, the man who'd used the axe to save her. Maybe the king was right, maybe they were one and the same, a were-bear.

Marlene hadn't gone far when she heard a shot in the distance. She picked up the pace. Sound carried well in the mountains and it took a while to locate the source of the gunfire. She found a man with a rifle cowering behind an old truck. He was trembling and obviously had soiled himself.

"What happened here?" she asked.

"B-b-b-bear, big fucking bear. Big as a house bear... Nice tits. What happened to your shirt, girl? Come here and tell me about it."

With a sigh Marlene realized she was naked to the waist as she'd discarded the shirt and bra ruined by the shotgun blast. "I went skinny dipping in the river to escape the heat. Damn kids stole my clothes. I chased them and got it all back except my shirt. I don't suppose you have a spare with you?"

"No. Look, girl, you should be a long way from here with that giant bear on the loose." He rose, and leering at her, took a step closer. "I managed to wing it, but a wounded bear is nothing to play with, especially one this big. Say, what kids were you talking about? There's nobody living anywhere near here, and there's no river..."

"Be silent."

Unable to speak, the man watched in horror while the beautiful naked girl changed into a monster. He tried to get up and run, but she was on him, fangs biting deep. He whimpered and struggled then went limp in her arms. She tossed him aside then licked her lips and slowly morphed back into the girl.

"Give me your shirt." Trembling, he took it off and passed it to her. She slipped it on then tied it up under her breasts. *"Go home now and*

clean yourself up. You will not remember me at all. You shot at a bear then went home. That's all you will remember. Go now!"

The shaken and terrified man scrambled to his feet, climbed into the truck, and drove away. She watched him go until the truck disappeared from sight, then turned her attention to the trail again. She had fed, she had a shirt, and she had a blood trail to follow. Things were looking up.

The trail led through some rough ground, and it was growing dark quickly, but the vampire was on a blood trail now. The clouds began to gather, further hampering her progress, but she continued on. She broke from the trees to see a small farm just as the skies opened up.

Marlene raced for the barn and slipped inside out of the rain, but now she was soaked. A soaking wet cat is not a happy creature, and neither is a soaking wet vampire. Ah well, there was fresh hay. Marlene burrowed into the haystack and sighed, memories of her childhood in France flooding her mind, brought on by the scent of fresh hay.

Marlene had been born to a poor peasant farmer, the middle child of seven daughters. There wasn't enough room for all in the hut, so several of the girls slept in the barns with the livestock. With another deep sigh she relaxed, allowing the hay to insulate her and hold her body heat in, in spite of her clothes being soaked. Six hundred years and more of living in relative luxury vanished as the peasant girl drifted off to sleep.

Awakening with the dawn, she yawned and stretched then rose to her feet. She was completely healed and well fed, time to get back on the trail. Marlene would track the bear until the sun was higher then she would rest until dusk, at least that was the plan.

It didn't work out that way, the heavy rains had washed away any signs of a blood trail and she couldn't catch any hint of the bear's scent. She was still in the barnyard, swearing like a trooper and picking straws of hay from her hair, when the old farmer came towards the barn.

"Mornin' girl. You lost?"

"Hello there. Yes, I guess I am lost. I got separated from the others and took shelter in your barn for the night. Hope you don't mind."

He paused for a moment as he got a good look at her, alarm bells going off in his head. "Don't mind a bit, but I gotta tell you, this isn't a really friendly area, especially for strangers. You look like a city gal to me. Got a car nearby someplace?"

Marlene grinned. "Yes, I'm a city girl, and yes I do have a car, but I have no idea how to get back to where I left it."

"Can you tell me about the place?"

"It's just outside Warrenville, big parking lot near a small lake."

"That's a fair bit away from here, gal. Tell you what, as soon as I feed my stock I'll give you a ride back to your car. There're some bad actors around these parts, a city gal alone could get into trouble real easy. Come on, let's get these hogs fed then get you back to your car."

The old fellow continued to chat away as he fed the stock, gathered the eggs, then fetched the keys to his aging pickup truck. He'd offered to cook her breakfast, but she'd said she was in a hurry to get home so off they went. Over an hour later they reached her car. The windows had been smashed in.

"Dirty bastards," muttered the old fellow. "Hope you didn't leave any valuables in that car."

"I did. I just hope they didn't find them." Marlene got out and pulled the keys from the pocket of her jeans. She popped the trunk and reached inside. Marlene flipped the hidden switch and they heard a latch pop. She opened the back door and looked inside the hidden compartment. Her phone, ID, and a small roll of money were still there.

"Pretty slick," grinned the old fellow.

"Yeah, my ex-boyfriend was a drug smuggler. Okay, I'll call AAA to come get the car. Can I give you some money for gas and your trouble?"

"That's not necessary, girl. Look, I can see you're no ordinary hiker. I have to tell ya, folks in these hills don't take kindly to government agents poking around, if you get my drift."

"Thanks for the warning," replied Marlene, "but I'm not a government agent."

"Ah huh, if you say so. I've got to get back to the farm. Will you be all right here until the tow truck comes?"

"I'll be fine, thanks. Sure you won't take any money for gas?"

"No, girl, just pass the favor along to the next poor soul you find in trouble."

"I'll do that. Say, what's your name, my savior?"

"Bill Walker, at your service, ma'am."

"It's a pleasure to have met you, Mr. Walker. I'm Marlene de France." He smiled and waved as he drove away.

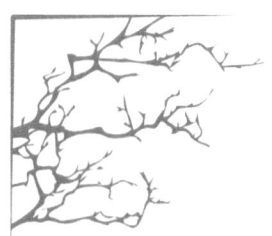

Starting Over

Marlene sat in the car staring at her cell phone. There was no help for it, she had to check in. With a deep sigh she punched in the numbers hoping no one would be awake at this hour. It was answered on the third ring. "Marlene?"

"Yes, Sire, it is I. You're awake late."

"I've been waiting for your call. What the hell happened?"

"I got sloppy, I got killed, and I lost the bear's trail. He's been wounded, but I have no idea if he heals as quickly as we do. Worse, when I managed to revive myself and get back to my car it had been vandalized. It's now been repaired and I'm on my way back to start over."

"Marlene, you do remember how this is done, don't you? It's only been a few hundred years since the Sweden adventure after all." The mirth in his voice truly irritated her.

"Yes, Harald, I remember how this is done."

"You sound upset, Marlene," he chuckled.

"I am upset, and more. Tell me there's no rule against killing that damned bear."

"Only if you must. Try to find out what he truly is, and if there are more of them, before you make a new rug for your quarters."

"You're having far too much fun at my expense, Harald."

"I could ask Georg to help you track him."

She sighed. "No, the people around here would shoot the wolf for his pelt, and they'll shoot the man for being a stranger. I'll handle it myself."

"All right, Marlene. All joking aside, we can get help to you if you need it. Stay in touch." With that he was gone.

"Sweden? So that's how it is, is it, Harald. All right then, so be it."

She started the car and set out for Bill Walker's farm. As the miles rolled by Marlene cast her mind back over the centuries, to that hunt for the mad Finnlander. The man had been only human, but he was like a will-o-the-wisp in the forest, especially in winter.

He'd surprised a group of travelers, robbed and murdered them. Among them had been a young nobleman and his mistress, Marlene. Even though Marlene had lived centuries in luxury by then, she still remembered the hard life she'd lived as a child. She'd revived, dressed in the clothes of a dead guardsman, and gone after the mad Finn.

For over two years she tracked that madman through the snowy forests of Scandinavia and Russia until she finally caught up with him. He had nearly fifty heavily armed men with him when she found them, but she killed them all and retrieved the golden pendant her lover had given her. She still had it.

Yes, Marlene could track in the forests, and she could go to war if necessary, she just didn't like it. She'd rather go shopping in Paris. Goddamn fucking bear was going to pay for her losing her vacation.

She rolled into the barnyard just at sunrise. The old farmer was just on his way to feed the hogs. "Woman, what the merry hell are you doing back here?"

"Hey there, friend of mine. I need a favor."

"A favor?"

"I need to put the car someplace for a few days where it won't get trashed. Can I hide it in your barn?"

"You running from the law?"

"Nope."

"Are you the law?"

"Oh hell no."

"All right then, you can hide it in the barn." He watched as she put the car inside and locked it up then tossed him the keys. "Girl, what the hell is going on?"

"I'd tell you, Bill, but then I'd just have to shoot you."

"Right. Look, you should stay out of the woods for a few days. Some dang fool wounded a bear, now there's hunters and dogs everywhere. Them morons will shoot at anything that moves. Even if they don't get you, a wounded bear is nothing to sneeze at."

He cocked his head and looked more closely at her. "My god, it's the bear you're after, ain't it? Girl, what the hell are you? You're one of them, aren't you?"

"One of them?"

"I saw a man with eyes like yours back in Germany in the war. Next day I saw him get killed then stand up and bite the enemy. Oh dear sweet baby Jesus, you really are like him." He was backing away, but she just leaned against the rail.

"What did he look like, this man you saw?"

Bill stopped backing away and gave her a puzzled look. "Stocky fella, dark hair, in a Russian uniform."

"Hmm, Peter most likely. I take it he didn't see you."

"Nope, he sure didn't. So, you are like him, can't be killed, drinks blood."

"Yes."

"Vampire."

"Yes."

He swallowed hard then squared his shoulders. "Ah well, what the hell, I'm old as dirt anyway. Go ahead, get it over with."

She moved then, a feminine figure moving with liquid grace, exuding power and danger. As she reached him Marlene took him by the shoulders. "I'm not going to hurt you, you're my friend, you were kind to me. However, I do want your promise to keep my secret."

He nodded then swallowed hard again. "Did you kill the Emory Brothers with the axe? Everybody says it was their young cousin Deke, but..."

"No, that wasn't me, Bill. I don't kill people if I can help it. Dead bodies are too hard to explain away."

"Good to know," he said, as he sighed with relief. "It's coming light now; you should probably hide out in the barn until dark. It's gonna be a hot one."

"Not a bad idea at that, Bill. I'll nap in the hay until nightfall then disappear into the woods."

"All right, you get some rest and I'll pretend you were never here."

She chuckled as she headed back inside the barn out of the direct sun. When he checked at dusk she was already gone. By the time it was fully dark she was back where the man had shot the bear, casting about for any sign of a blood trail. What she found was the scent and tracks of several men and dogs.

All through the night and well into the next day she followed them, slowly gaining on the hunters. Eventually she took shelter from the sun and caught a few hours sleep in a shallow cave. At dusk she was back on the trail. It was full dark when she heard them swearing.

Watching from the forest, she saw them standing on the banks of a broad lake. The bear had taken to the water. Listening carefully she learned the bear had entered the water, but the dogs couldn't find where it had come out. Frustrated and angry they called for a ride home.

While the hunters and dogs returned to the nearest roadway to wait for their ride, the vampire searched the lake shore. The scent was cold, but still a trace of it lingered there. Eventually she found it. It wasn't the scent of the bear she found; it was the scent of the man with the axe.

The clouds covered the moon and stars, and even the night vision of a vampire couldn't penetrate the gloom. Marlene sat beneath a tree and waited for the dawn. When light returned to the world she took up the trail again. According to the tracks, the man was limping.

She was surprised that he didn't head for the nearest town. Instead he'd headed deeper into the forest. She continued to track him by scent and sight until dusk. He was no longer limping, but she'd gained on him. Darkness fell as the scent and tracks turned from those of a man to those of a bear. Marlene began to curse as the tracks showed the bear was running.

"So it's going to be like this is it? Fine. The ground is getting too rough to be tracking in the dark. Might as well get some sleep." With that in mind Marlene settled down beneath a tree, wishing she were back in her apartment, or at least in Bill's barn. Hopefully it wouldn't rain again.

It didn't rain, but the dawn brought another problem. Marlene needed to feed. She picked up the bear's trail easily and set out, but far slower than she would have liked. She was getting hungry. Keeping a sharp eye out for unwary prey, she stayed on the bear's trail until the sun got too high. Tired, hungry, and wanting a shower, Marlene slunk into the shade of the trees to wait for sundown.

WHILE THE VAMPIRE SETTLED down to rest, another woman awakened, terrified. She was looking down at the ground so far away. It took several moments for her to realize she wasn't falling. Not understanding what was happening, she tried to call for help, but the only sound that came from her throat was the cry of a hawk.

THE VAMPIRE SAT WITH her back to a tree, gently tapping the back of her head against the rough bark and lamenting her fate. If she'd just gone to the airport she would now be in Paris now, shopping, the theater, ... but no, she'd had to say one last good-bye to show off her new outfit. She'd barely entered the great hall when the king had spotted her.

"Ah, Marlene, I'm glad you're still here."

"Harald?"

"Something's come up."

"Oh no you don't, I have to be at the airport in two hours ..."

"Marlene, I'm sorry, and I swear I'll make it up to you, but there's nobody else."

She'd sighed then and accepted her fate. If she'd had any idea at all of what was coming she'd have made more of a fuss. "All right, Sire, what is it?"

"There's been some unusual killings in the hill country south of here. It's not a vampire, but something else, perhaps a rogue werewolf, but I don't think so. There are stories of a giant bear that can appear and disappear at will. There's quite a hue and cry going on, dozens of hunters everywhere."

"So, you suspect a non-human?"

"We dare not take that chance, Marlene, you know this."

Again she'd sighed. "What's the mission?"

"Discover if it's truly a non-human. If so, bring it here until we can find sanctuary for it."

"If it doesn't want to come?"

"Then kill it and dispose of the remains. Above all, the human population must remain unaware of our existence. You can take Georg with you."

"No, Sire, the hunters of that area would kill the wolf just for sport. No, I'll do this, but ..."

"Would six weeks in Paris be sufficient?" he'd asked with a grin.

"It's a start," she'd replied. Marlene had returned to her apartment, changed into hiking clothes, then set out for the hill country.

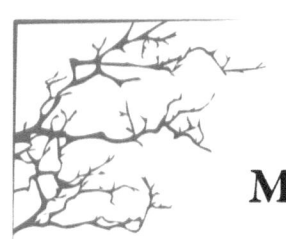

Mistaken Identity

As the sun dropped low over the hills Marlene set out again. The scent was faint, but easily followed. She hadn't gone too far when she found where the bear had stopped to feed. "So, you're as hungry as I am, are you? And I no longer smell blood; you've healed yourself. Good to know. Now, I need to find blood, and soon."

Keeping an eye out for likely game, she continued along, following the trail of the bear. She was getting closer, for it had stopped often to feed. "Ha, so the big bear has a big belly to fill," she grinned. "Healing takes energy, as I well know. You'll have to sleep soon, my furry friend. Perhaps I'll catch up to you in the night."

She had already shifted into killing mode. The half tiger ghosted along, following the bear's trail, when suddenly she caught a different scent. Humans. Somehow hunters had crossed the bear's trail. A snarl crossed her feline features as she shifted her focus from one form of prey to another.

The sound of shots mixed with the roar of the bear reached her ears and she leaped forward. She found two dead and one wounded hunter. Battering aside his rifle she sank her fangs into his throat and drank greedily. Finally she thrust him away, sated at last, yet fighting the killing lust.

Weakly the man reached for and retrieved his fallen rifle. She heard the click as he wrenched a fresh shell into the chamber and pulled the trigger. The vampire's lightning fast reflexes saved her from harm. Again she batted aside the weapon then attacked. This time it wasn't her fangs, but her claws he faced.

18

He tried to scream as the claws ripped into him, ending his life, but he failed. To any who found them it would look like the bear had killed them all. She leaped into the branches of a tree and swung out onto exposed rock. Again she set out after the bear. Once more she had a fresh blood trail to follow.

By dawn she'd cornered the bear, or so she thought. The scent was fresh, and she could hear the beast's labored breathing. Moving cautiously, she closed in. Just as she drew close enough to reach out and touch the animal, the ground gave way from under her. Marlene screamed as she fell.

She had no idea how far the fall might have been, she just thanked the gods of fortune she'd hit a tree and grabbed a branch. She had a few scrapes, but they were healing almost instantly. Fortunately she was well fed, had she not been, she might have been far more seriously hurt.

As she secured her perch in the tree, and swearing softly, she heard a voice from above. "You'll never get me, Mobutu, I thought you'd have learned by now. I'm too smart for you."

"I'm not Mobutu, you fucking moron," she shouted in reply. "Mobutu would have killed you by now."

"So the coward sends his minions to do the work he can't manage. Still won't help you, woman. Leave off or I'll finish you. Go back to that madman and leave me alone."

"Mobutu is dead. I'm not one of his minions, I serve the Vampire King. I just want to talk to you."

Marlene looked up to see a face peering over the edge of the bluff. It was a man, but the like of which she had never seen outside a museum. His hair was thick, dark, and he was bearded. He had thick eyebrow ridges and strong looking jaws. As he leaned out to get a better look at her she could see the powerful muscles of his shoulders and arms. He had a fairly thick coat of body hair. Yes, it was the man with the axe.

"What do you want?"

"Excuse me?"

"You said you wanted to talk, what do you want?"

"Out of this damned tree for starters, then to sit down together and talk like civilized people. I want to know all about you."

"You mean learn my weaknesses so you can kill me."

"I already know your weaknesses, you paranoid fool. I know you stay in bear mode as much as possible because you have trouble passing for human in this day and age. I know it takes a lot more food to keep you going as the bear than it would as a man. I also know that humans have clued in to you, are trying to capture or kill you, and we have to prevent that."

"You want to keep me alive? Why?"

"Try to understand, if the humans discover what you are, they'll hunt and kill you, or worse. Moreover, if they get you they'll know that non-humans exist. That means they'll start hunting for others. They'll hunt us all into extinction. That's why I want to keep you alive and get you far away from here."

"I can take care of myself; they'll never catch me."

"Oh yeah, you're doing a bang up job of that all right. You've killed half a dozen people in the past two months."

"They think a bear did it."

"Yes, and they want that bear dead. There are dozens of hunters with rifles, dogs, and god knows what else, on your trail. It's just a matter of time before they get you."

"I can take care of myself," replied the man as his face disappeared from sight. Marlene could hear him moving away.

It was full daylight and, still swearing in three languages, Marlene descended from the tree that had saved her. She'd learned some things about this creature, but not enough. Yes, it was definitely a were-bear, but from a bygone age. She suspected he was a cave bear, old, not as old as Ella, but older than Harald or even older than Mobutu had been.

He also knew about vampires, for he'd thought it was Mobutu on his trail. He spoke English well enough, so he'd lived among humans in the recent past, but something had set him on the run and a killing spree. She had to catch up with him again and learn more.

So far, Harald wasn't going to like any of this, and Marlene wasn't certain how easy this bear would be to kill. Even the tigress would have trouble with this big boy.

No, if she decided she had to kill him, she'd have to catch him in human form. That wouldn't be easy to do. It was a slow tough climb back to the ridge and his trail. He was still wounded, for she could smell the blood trail. Marlene decided to push him hard, tire him out, and maybe get him to talk some more.

Staying out of the direct sun as much as possible, Marlene followed the fleeing bear, for he was once again traveling in bear form. The sun was high overhead and the scent stronger when she found the hunting party.

In a small clearing stood a man with a rifle, beside him another sat weeping and rocking the dead body in his arms. The scent of blood was almost overpowering, and Marlene still needed to feed. Fighting that maddening desire to kill, to feed, she approached the men. "What happened here?"

The man with the rifle turned and aimed at her, then lowered his weapon. Before him stood a slim girl with reddish brown hair and a light dusting of freckles across her pale skin. She smiled reassuringly as she approached. "Who the hell are you and what are you doing here?"

"I was hiking and got lost. What happened here?"

"That goddamn bear killed my son, sobbed the man on the ground. "It came out of the trees right at us, killed poor Jody, then ran off. Damn thing is big as a house. It's tryin' to destroy my whole family."

"Now, John, that's crazy talk. That monster's a rogue bear, Miss. It's a killer. You can come with us. We need to get outta here right now."

The man on the ground tenderly lowered the dead man then stood up. "We ain't going nowhere until that bear's dead. It killed two of my sons and my sister's boy plus young Tommy. I'm serious, Donnie. We ..."

He got no further as Marlene lost the battle with the blood lust. She battered aside the rifle and leaped on the grieving father, her fangs biting deep, a moan of pure pleasure escaping her as the hot blood spurted into her mouth. She drank deep, all the while holding the other man transfixed with her eyes.

Trembling and whimpering with fear, he struggled to bring his rifle to bear. She thrust her victim aside and leaped at him. He got off a shot before she reached him, but he missed in his panic. Again she bit deep and drank. A few moments of pure joy as the blood filled her mouth and sated her need, then she thrust him away.

By this time her first victim had regained his own rifle. He raised it to shoot as she turned back to him. The sight of her made him pause in confusion. The half cat was taller with a leonine face, long muscular arms, and large hands tipped with razor sharp claws. Before he could react she moved, snatching away the weapon and tossing it aside.

"You're both still alive for the moment. Be still, talk to me, and you'll remain that way. Attempt anything else and the bear will have left more than one victim in this clearing." For emphasis she flexed her hands, showing her claws. Both men swallowed hard and backed away from her.

They tried to run but a voice from a distant hell stopped them cold. "*Stop. Come back here.*" Terrified, and fighting the compulsion all the way, they none the less returned to face the vampire. "*Remain here and talk to me until I give you permission to go.*"

Both men swallowed hard as they watched the creature shimmer back into the pretty girl with the freckles. "Now, you said the bear was targeting your family, yes?"

"That's right."

"Any idea why?"

"None at all."

"Unless," said the other man.

"Unless what?"

"Well, Miss, it just seems weird, that's all. A few weeks ago John's boys went to work for Paul Hardy. A bunch of them went with him to clear old Widow Martin off her land. They beat up that half baked field hand of hers then ran him off. They then beat up and killed her claiming the field hand did it, but everybody knows the difference.

"People say she was a witch and her spirit put a spell that bear to get revenge."

"Donnie, that's pure horse shit and you know it."

"Is it, John? Then you tell me why the hell that giant bear is killing all your kin. Hell, girl, he broke from the trees, went right past me and John to get to the boy. Ripped him apart then took off. I winged him, but that's all."

"That field hand, what did he look like?"

"Torvil? Well, he's about five eight, sturdy, and strong as a mule, hairy as a dog, black hair, real heavy eyebrows, sort of looks like a caveman. He don't talk much, but he watches everything. They tried to find him after the killin' was done, but he'd managed to crawl away and hide. Nobody's seen him since. Some folks say the witch's spirit changed him into the bear and sent him out to get revenge.

"Hell, might even be true at that, cause the damned thing can't be killed. Several of us have had a clear shot at it, but it just won't go down. It's an evil spirit, I tell you, and I'm done trying to hunt it."

"This is all bullshit, Donnie, and you know it. My boys wouldn't have anything to do with a thing like that. Yes, I know, Doris Martin was beaten and killed in her own house, but I think that freak Torvil done it. That's why he disappeared."

"*That's enough,*" came that frightening voice. "*Listen carefully, the bear attacked your party, killed the boy, then vanished into the trees. You managed to wound it, but that's all. You then gathered up the body and returned home. You saw no one else in this clearing, just the bear. Go now, take the body home and forget about hunting the bear. It's a spirit bear and cannot be killed.*"

The two men shook off the spell. "Damn, John, I'm truly sorry about young Jody. Come on, I'll help you get him back to the truck."

"No, you carry the rifles, Donnie. I'll carry my son." Both men completely ignored the young woman standing in the clearing with them. Slowly, sadly, they left, carrying their dead companion with them.

High overhead a hawk had watched the people in the clearing. The woman changing into the monster and back again had caught her attention.

Marlene, now well fed and ready for the hunt once again, turned and set out on the trail of the bear. Her face was hot, and her nose felt like it was burned from the sun. If she had a sunburn that damned bear was going to pay. She felt an itch on her nose and started to swear.

Lying back beneath the shade of an old oak, and watching a large hawk overhead watching her, Marlene took the time to heal her sunburn before resuming the hunt. When she did, the hawk followed.

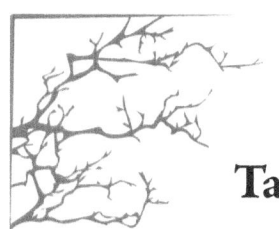

Talking to the Bear

The day was nearly over before she caught up with the bear again. This time it was different, the blood trail led right up to a cave and inside. Marlene shifted to vampire mode as she cautiously stepped inside and waited until her eyes adjusted to the gloom. There was the bear, badly wounded and braced against the back of the cave. It was huge and snarled while lifting a warning paw.

"Easy now, big boy, I'm not here to hurt you. I can be a friend if you let me." Slowly she let her body return to human form and sat down, an easy target if the bear wanted to attack. "Looks like you're hurt pretty bad, right? Is there anything I can do to help?"

Slowly the bear shimmered into human form. "Go ahead, get it over with, but you won't get much blood from me. Not now."

"I told you before, I'm not here to hurt you, I just want to talk."

"Sure, fine. Don't suppose you've got anything to eat with you?"

"Not with me. Look, I can go hunting if the meat will help you heal."

"It will."

"Okay, but you'd better be here when I get back." She rose with the grace of a hunting cat, shimmering into killing mode, and vanished from the cave. A short while later she returned with a brace of rabbits. He was gone. The hawk was overhead, watching, but Marlene didn't seem to notice.

"Dirty rotten son of a bitch."

Marlene picked up the scent and went after him. It only took a few minutes to catch up, his wound had reopened, and he was bleeding freely again. He was back in bear form, so she tossed the rabbits to him

25

and waited while he fed. When finished he shimmered back to human form again.

"I didn't expect you to come back."

"I expected you to be there when I did. You have some serious trust issues, Mr. Bear."

"I suppose I do at that," he chuckled. "All right, you keep saying you want to talk, and you did bring me food, so, what's on your mind?"

"Mostly my apartment in Paris and a hot bath with scented candles."

"Ah-huh."

"Like I said before, I work for the vampire king. You started killing every human in sight, so he called off my vacation and sent me after you. So tell me, why the killings?"

"Those bastards deserved what they got."

"I'm not arguing that, just asking why."

"They beat and killed my wife."

"Your wife?"

"About seventy odd years ago I met a girl named Doris. She was the sweetest person you could meet, cute as a button too. Most people take one look at me and run away, or think I'm stupid, or worse. Idiots. Doris looked past that and liked what she found. She was only eighteen, but we married that spring and moved north.

"About five years ago we moved to this area and changed our story as she was in her eighties. I pretended to be the hired hand. One night a car pulled into the yard. I went out to see what was going on and got flattened. Guy hit me from behind with a rifle butt. The second one put me out cold. I thought I heard her screaming.

"I came to and found her, what they'd done to her. I got their scent then the bear went hunting."

"So you weren't saving me from a fate worse than death when you killed those two with the axe?"

"Two birds with one stone, as they say. I saved you from a fate like my poor Dorrie, and got two of the bastards who hurt her. It works for me."

"So, have you got them all now?"

"Nope, there's one more."

"You sure?"

"Woman, I got the scent of every man from her tortured body. There's one more."

"All right, can't say I blame you for any of it, but now there's a problem, a number of them in fact."

"Oh?"

"Yes, point number one, your killing spree is drawing far too much undesired attention, and it's getting harder and harder for me to cover it up."

"Cover it up? You're covering it up? Why the hell are you doing that? I want these bastards exposed for what they did."

"Not going to happen, my friend," sighed Marlene. "See, here's the problem, you draw too much attention and get caught, your true nature exposed to the world, humans freak out, go hunting for, and start killing, every non-human they can find. You've lived among them long enough to know that's what'll happen. That's why the king sent me to find you."

"You mean to kill me."

"No, that's the last thing he wants. That's the last resort. The king wants to meet you, learn about you, and probably help you find a place of sanctuary."

"Sanctuary?"

"Yes. The king would far rather keep you alive."

The man stared thoughtfully into the small campfire for a long moment. "What are some of the other issues?"

"You're hurt badly, and it takes you a lot longer to heal than it does me."

He sighed deeply and poked at the fire. "Can't argue that."

"All right, let's work from there. Will you let me help you?"

"Help me what?"

"Find a place of safety to heal. While you're healing I can contact the king, and we can work from there." He didn't respond for a long moment so she changed into full vampire mode. "Look at me, Torvil." He looked up, startled at what he saw. "Like you, I'm not human either. As one non-human to another, let me help you."

"If I say no, are you going to kill me?"

"No, but I might kick your sorry ass a few times to beat some sense into that thick head of yours."

That actually made him laugh. "All right, but only if you change back into the pretty girl, you're scary as hell like that."

Grinning with delight, Marlene changed back. "Deal. Okay, now tell me what you need to speed up the healing."

"More meat and a couple of days," he replied. "Normally it wouldn't take so long, but I was already wounded when I got shot the last time."

"Okay, I get that. I'll go hunting in the morning. So, can you resurrect completely as we do?"

"Come back from the dead? Yes, as long as my body doesn't get butchered or dismembered, at least I think so. I've come back a few times, but I'm god awful hungry and weak when I do. How about you?"

"Hungry. When it happens the need for blood is so powerful it's maddening. By drinking the blood of a human I can mimic their appearance. I take it you can't?"

"Nope. This is what most people looked like when I became the bear. Near as I can figure it, my father was a Homo Sapien and mother was a Neanderthal. Lots of us in the clan at that time. I've tried, but what you see is what you get."

She smiled and nodded. "Yeah, I read somewhere that the two species interbred at one point in time. Any idea how you became the bear?"

"I'd just become clan leader at the death of my father during a hunt. I was searching for a suitable cave for the clan when I happened on the bear. He was a monster and came at me. His first blow nearly killed me and he tried again. I dodged away and his claws struck a rock which exploded into a green dust, killing him and nearly me.

"When I woke up I crawled out from under the bear's carcass and went looking for the clan. When I found them they had a new guy as leader. He didn't want to give up the job and he came at me. He hurt me and I changed, became the bear and killed him, a few more of the clan as well, then ran away.

"I've been on my own for a long time, joined a few human settlements, even married a couple of times, but as they evolve it's getting harder to do."

"I get that. So, you eventually gained control of the change."

"That took a while. In those days it was hard to hunt on your own, feed yourself. I managed to survive until I mastered the change then it got a lot easier. Eventually I reached the point where I can hold my mind clear even when in bear form."

"So, when did you encounter Mobutu?"

"Oh, that was a long time ago. It was in Europe, I think. Anyway, he saw me change and went crazy. I barely had time to change back into the bear. He ranted and raved on about being the only god, and that all others must die. He came at me a few times and I killed him every time. The last time he revived to find me watching him. I tore him apart and scattered the pieces thinking I'd made an end of him at last."

"You say he's dead for sure?"

"Yes, the king defeated him but didn't manage to kill him, so he captured the queen. We all went after him. Mother killed him, and then they cremated the body and spread the ashes, some on the plains and some in the ocean. Mobutu's not coming back from that one.

"All right, I've badgered you enough for one night. You get some rest and I'll keep watch. I'll go hunting in the morning." She noticed a hawk perched in a tree and wondered if she'd seen it before.

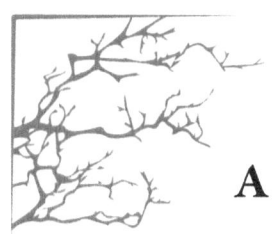

A Tale for the King

"Majesty, it's Marlene," said Tommy, as he hit the speaker button and set the phone where all could hear.

"Marlene, where are you? What's the situation?"

"Sire, I'm halfway up a tree on a hilltop. Reception in these areas isn't easy to find. The situation is as follows. I've made contact with the were-bear. I estimate he's at least fifty thousand years old, probably more. The bear is a large cave bear. The man is a homo-sapien / Neanderthal hybrid. He can heal himself as we do, and return from the lands beyond as we do, but he's unable to alter his appearance to mimic modern humans as we do. His current name is Torvil, he's strong as an ox, extremely intelligent, stubborn as a mule, and has taken pains to educate himself.

"He went on a killing spree because his wife, who was in her eighties, was beaten and killed to gain title to her lands. By this time, Torvil was pretending to be the hired hand, and he was blamed for the murder. He's managed to kill all but one of the perpetrators and is hell bent on finishing the last one before he does anything else.

"He's sleeping now, healing from a gunshot through the back. Harald, I really don't want to kill this man. I doubt if I could anyway, but ..."

"I do understand, Marlene. I'd feel the same way and do the same thing if anything ever happened to my Sally. I want to talk to this fellow, and I need time to confer with the others. I agree, killing him is not the desired option. We need a bit of time to find a solution, and a few options for him to consider. Killing him will be a last resort. Can you keep him out of trouble for a while?"

Marlene sighed deeply. "I'll try, Sire, but it'll be no easy task."

"So, what's the king's verdict?"

"You heard me?"

"Bears have good hearing, besides, there's only one reason for you to climb a tree at the top of a hill. You were looking for phone reception."

"Maybe I was calling my boyfriend."

"No, I don't believe that."

"Why not?"

"You've been on my trail for quite a while. If you had a boyfriend you'd have checked in long before now."

Marlene laughed, and that brought a grin of delight to his face. "Busted. Yes, I reported in to the king. He says he wants to talk to you, and he wants me to keep you out of trouble until he confers with his advisers."

"Good luck with that one. Got any ideas how you're supposed to keep me out of trouble?"

"Only one."

"Care to share with the old bear?"

"I'd like to hide you with a friend while I find and kill the last man on your list."

That caught his attention. He stepped closer and gazed deeply into her eyes. "Why would you do that?"

"You stand out in a crowd, Torvil. That's neither a bad thing nor a good thing, but it is what it is. Number two, everybody with a dog or a gun is hunting for you, both in human and bear form. They don't know the difference, but again, it is what it is. Number three, I have a strong feeling you'll be more reasonable when talking to the king if that man is dead, your vengeance complete."

Torvil sighed and sat back down. "You're not wrong about that, girl. I wanted to kill him myself, make sure he knew why it was happening, but I guess as long as he's dead I'll be content."

"He'll know, Torvil. I promise, he'll know, admit his guilt first, then he'll know why he's going to die. So, is it a deal?"

"Girl, where the hell do you expect to find somebody dumb enough to hide me?"

"I know a guy," she grinned. "So, is it a deal?"

"All right, if you're serious, it's a deal."

"Excellent, so, what's the man's name and where do I find him?"

"His name's Paul Hardy. He's a local land grabber and money hog. Our property had the misfortune of lying in the path of an oncoming oil pipeline. Hardy got wind of the route and started strong arming everybody who owned property in its path. We wouldn't sell."

"Why not?"

"My Dorrie loved that old house, all the roses growing outside and the sweet water well. She wanted to spend her remaining years there. I wanted to make that happen for her, but Hardy started getting nasty. He said I was nothing but a half-breed retard of a hired hand, and I should have no say in the matter. I threw him off the property, physically, and he didn't take it well."

"So he came back with a crew of hired thugs?"

"Yes. I got slugged from behind and the rest you know."

"Where do I find this Paul Hardy?"

"He's got an office over in Jonasville, but he's rarely there."

"All right, I'll start there."

"Are you sure about killing this man? Can you do it?"

"Oh for Christ's sake. Listen you, I spent over a hundred years working as an assassin, and in the process I kept myself well fed and built up quite a fortune. As far as I'm concerned, we have a contract. I'll live up to my end and you live up to yours.

"Now, do you know of a man named Bill Walker?"

"Walker, Walker, oh yeah, old fella, lives over near Tompson's Ridge."

"Yes, that's Bill. We'll go to his place. I'm sure I can talk him into hiding you for a few days."

"You're serious?"

"I am."

"All right, but I think we should wait until tomorrow by the looks of those clouds. There's a sweet little cave just over there where we can wait out the storm."

"Lead on, Mr. Bear," grinned Marlene. He rose easily and started to climb the hill. She followed close behind, the hawk following high above.

A King's Concern

While Marlene and the were-bear settled down in a cave to wait out the storm, the king of the vampires sat brooding on his throne, as he called the huge office chair at the head of the long table. The queen found him there and slipped an arm around his shoulders. She kissed his cheek and sighed. "It's all right, Harald. I don't mind moving, and I'll happily go wherever you want to take me."

That brought a smile to his lips, and he hugged her gently. "So, snooping around in my head again, are you?"

"I can't help it, lover. I've always been keenly attuned to you, your moods. Ever since you marked me as your own it's like I feel everything you do, know your every thought. You're thinking of leaving America, aren't you?"

"Yes. The political situation is getting far too volatile here just as it did in Germany in the thirties. For a solitary vampire it would be no problem, a blessing even, but I am solitary no longer. I have the rest of my kin, all our human allies, Illya's people, and now the were-bear to consider.

"This warehouse complex was never meant to be a permanent home for us, it was merely a convenient temporary set up in a rich hunting ground for we vampires. Now, with more non-humans and humans as well, we need something more elaborate and something more easily secured. Frankly, people, we need a lair that is defensible.

"Tommy, has everyone returned?"

"Everybody's checked in, Sire, except Marlene."

"All right, call them in, we need to get this out in the open and discuss it. I need to know how the rest of you feel about this. See if you can get Illya on conference call as well."

"I'm on it, Sire," replied Tommy, as his fingers began to fly across his keyboard. Soon cryptic messages began to reach people scattered throughout the city. The vampires began to gather.

Once everyone had gathered in the conference room the king called the great hall, Queen Sally went to find him. He was in the exercise room practicing with his two-handed great sword. Sweat ran freely from his brow and he was grinning with delight. Somehow swordplay always seemed to help him clear his mind.

Harald was mopping his brow as he entered the great hall and took his seat. "Tommy, have we got Illya on the line?"

"I am here, Great King," came a voice from the phone stand on the table.

"Excellent. All right, people, I won't mince words here. With the political situation in this country being what it is, I'm getting nervous. I'm starting to feel exposed here in the middle of this endless city. Exposed and under siege. I'd like to hear your thoughts on this."

Peter's deep chuckle was the first heard. "So, my king, you want to head off to Europe, find an abandoned castle near a forest, but close to a city, where we can start over."

"Yes, Peter, that's what I'd like to do. Listen now people, we have the Children of the Wolf to consider, and now Marlene has found us a were-bear. This man's human appearance creates another issue that would be easier to deal with in Europe.

"Worse yet, I fear we'll find others, some will be able to fit in with the humans as we do, but still many others won't be able to. We need a place with a more natural environment for those who need it, still more civilized environs for those of us who prefer that, and yet many places of secrecy where we can provide a sanctuary for still others."

"And there is still more to consider, Sire."

"Gudrun?"

"We need to be able to keep our operations free from prying eyes. There are certain elements around here getting too curious about this place, its comings and goings. We'll need a way to hide the plane as well as our personal movements, yet we'll need to feed ourselves as well as our charges. I know of a few places in the mountains of eastern Europe that might meet our needs."

"I was actually thinking Britain," replied the king. "The language is roughly the same and that would make it easier for our American folk to adapt to."

"Sadly, Sire," spoke up one of the other vampires, "the political situation in Britain is not a lot better than it is here."

Harald nodded his head thoughtfully. "Illya, give me your thoughts on this."

"I am disturbed, Great King. We've been in these wonderful new homes you made for us barely two years, and yet already the curious are getting bolder. Twice in the past month the pack has been watched by the flying machines. What are those called again, Tommy?"

"Drones."

"Yes, by drones. Mister Tommy used his magic to bring down the first one, but another came a few days later. We've become afraid to change to wolf form in case someone is watching. Perhaps it is time we returned to the mountains of our homeland."

"Dammit, this world moves too fast for me," growled the king. "Just one damned crisis after the other, with no time to breathe between. Options, people? Opinions? Suggestions?"

A tall, stern looking, woman arose and began to pace around. "Perhaps, Sire, we may not have to move so far away. Allow me to share some of my family history. My grandfather was a man who was plagued by paranoia. He saw the way the world was going and took precautions."

"Amanda?"

"Sire, my grandfather was an extremely wealthy man, as well as a classic paranoid. He had a place like you described built a few hours north of here. The manor house will easily house all of us in comfort, there is mountainous terrain heavily forested behind and over a hundred acres of it belongs to the property.

"Below the house is a series of bomb shelters built to withstand a nuclear attack. He had it built to look like an English castle, complete with moat and what he called the dungeon, fortified storage rooms. The access road is still maintained by the state, but the property has been empty for years. There are a few acres of farmland between the castle and the highway.

"The place is deserted now, but the family still has title and maintains the grounds. We'd have to fix it up and install someone we could trust in the farm guarding the approach. Someone who could warn us of any snoopers in the area. We'd be within an hour of a city for hunting purposes. Also there's a small airstrip, with a hangar, on the property. Grandfather was a pilot."

Ella West smiled. "You actually look wistful when you speak of your grandfather, Amanda."

A rare smile crossed Amanda's lips. "He was the only human who gave a damn if I lived or died when I was a child. He raised me, and I watched him deteriorate and descend into the madness of total paranoia. He's still alive and living in an institution. I'm his sole heir and I also hold his power of attorney."

"Amanda?"

"The place is yours if you want it, Harald. Why do I work instead of living in luxury? Because I must know, is there is a way to help him. If not, perhaps I can stave off the same fate for myself."

Amanda found herself gently held in the arms of the queen. "Amanda..."

"It's all right, Sally. Being with the team, and lately with the royal court, I've learned to trust at a level I'd never hoped to achieve. I begin to suspect my own paranoia might be more from early childhood conditioning than from any other cause."

She returned the queen's hug then released her. "As I said, my lord, the place is yours if you want it."

"I'd really like to see it. Eric, find us comfortable transportation for six. Sally and I, Terry and Gudrun, and you and Amanda as well. We'll take a long look at this place from different perspectives.

"Gudrun, Eric, you will evaluate its military possibilities. Sally my heart, you and Amanda will evaluate its possibilities as living quarters for us all, plus more we may find ourselves with in future. Terry, you and I will explore its possibilities as housing etc. for other non-humans.

"Illya, do you want me to take Georg along or would you rather come yourself?"

"Take Georg with you. There is no time to wait for me. He is a clever and wise man who will one day become the alpha. I will trust his judgment."

"So be it. Eric..."

"The bus, Sire?"

"The bus, Eric," grinned Harald.

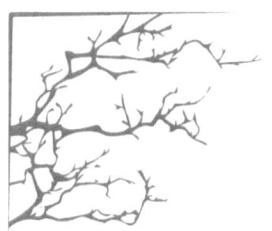

On the Hunt

While the king and company headed out in the luxury bus, Torvil awakened to find a grumpy vampire sharing the cave with him. The rain had stopped, the sun was out, but she didn't look happy. "You all right, girl?"

"I haven't had a bath or a meal in days, do I look all right to you?"

Thinking it best not to respond to that question he tried another tack. "There's a stream with a wide spot near her. It'd make a great swimming hole. Come on."

Fighting to get her temper under control, Marlene sighed and followed him closely. When they reached the spot she had to admit he'd been right. It was a perfect swimming hole. "All right now, I'll change into bear form and go forage. Take your time, have a bath, wash your clothes, find something to drink, and I'll come back later this afternoon."

"You're not going to run out on me are you?"

"Not much point in that. You'd just track me down anyway. No, girl, I'll come back. You do what you have to, and I'll see you later." With that he shifted into the bear and shambled away.

Marlene turned to the water hole to see a deer step out of the trees. Before the beast could understand there was danger the vampire slammed into it, knocking it to the ground. Sharp fangs sank deep and the poor creature's lifeblood spilled into her mouth. She drank greedily for a moment then thrust it away. The deer struggled to its feet and fled.

Greatly satiated, Marlene turned back and stripped off her clothes. With a leap and a shallow dive, she disappeared beneath the surface of the water causing barely a ripple. She swam lazily for a while, rubbing at her short hair and body. After a while she pulled her clothes in and washed them, then spread them out to dry, just as she had done as a girl so long ago.

While her clothes dried in the sun, Marlene dozed in the shade of a huge oak tree, watching the hawk overhead. The afternoon was wearing on when she heard the voices. "Well lookey there, Len, them's a girl's clothes spread out. Looks like she was in the water and got all wet."

He laughed at his own joke, but his friend was thoughtful. "Yeah, well, if that's the case then there's a nekked gal somewhere around here. We should take a look, you know, just to make sure she's all right." The other man snickered again, and they started casting about for any signs of a naked woman.

One man gave a startled squawk as he was hauled into a tree. His friend came running in time to see his limp body fall from the branches. "Len, Len, what the hell happened? Are you okay?"

The other man just groaned and tried to sit up. That's when the vampire stepped around the tree and grabbed his friend. Again she bit deep and drank greedily. Finally she thrust him aside as well. She seized up their rifles and hurled them into the woods, far away from their owners.

"What the fuck are you?"

"Be silent!"

Both men cringed back against the tree while she returned to her clothes and dressed herself. By this time she'd shimmered back into the girl instead of the half tiger. They were trying to crawl away when she returned for them, but they suddenly realized they were facing a gigantic bear. The bear growled and rose up on its back legs.

Terrified, the men turned and tried to flee in another direction, but the vampire was there. *"Stand still. Give me your car keys."* One man handed over the keys. *"Good, now, listen carefully. You came to this place, then fell asleep under a tree. You didn't see anybody, you did not see a bear. You have no idea what happened to your weapons or vehicle.*

Someone must have robbed you. You did not see me or the bear. Do you understand?"

Both men nodded fearfully. *"Very good, now lie down and go to sleep."* They obeyed.

"Come on, Torvil, we need to find their truck and get to Bill Walker's place." The bear turned and headed back into the trees. He soon arrived at a clearing with an old truck sitting there. He shimmered into the man as she unlocked the truck. Inside he found an old pair of boots and some coveralls. They were in business.

Marlene backed the truck out of the clearing and onto a dirt road. She soon reached the pavement and turned west. "If we're headed for Walker's place we're going the wrong way."

"Ah crap," she muttered, as she started looking for a spot to turn around. Eventually they got on the right road, and by dusk they reached Bill Walker's farm. There was a sign affixed to the door. Marlene started to swear as she read the eviction notice.

Bill came walking out of the barn, his head down. "Marlene, is that you?"

She went to him and took him by the shoulders. "What happened here?"

"Bank foreclosed," he replied softly. "My family's been on this land for generations. Ah, what the hell, I'm about done anyway. Glad you came back in time to get your car though. So, who's that with you?"

Marlene gave his shoulders a gentle squeeze then released him. "This is Torvil. Torvil, this is my friend, Bill Walker. Bill, I need you to hide Torvil for a few days."

"Sorry girl, can't help you there. I have to be off the land by noon tomorrow. They already came and hauled away my stock."

"Well that's not helpful," she replied with a snarl. "Hang on, I have to make a call." She walked a few steps toward the barn and pulled out her phone.

"Marlene?"

"Yes, Harald, it's me. A problem's come up."

"Tell me."

"I've brought Torvil, the were-bear, to a friend's place. He's refused to leave the area until he's killed the last man who harmed his wife. However, he's been accused of that crime himself and is now being hunted both as a bear and as a human. I brought him to Bill's farm with intentions of hiding him here while I personally assassinate the last of the killers."

"And the problem is?"

"I arrived to find an eviction notice on the door, and a friend with nowhere to go. Now I have two men to deal with and a grumpy were-bear to placate."

"What do you need?"

"What do you want me to do, Sire?"

"I want you to bring that were-bear to me and do it quietly. I don't care what else you have to do, just get this done."

"As you command, Sire."

With a half snarl Marlene broke the connection and returned the phone to her pocket. Glancing up she noticed the hawk soaring high above and snarled at it too. She went into the barn and brought her car out. Both men were still waiting where she'd left them. "We'll have to ditch that truck, it's a stolen vehicle. You guys follow me, and I'll dump it. You pick me up and we'll make another plan from there.

"Bill, have you family or friends to go to? Any other resources?"

"Nothing girl, the bank took it all. No family left alive. All I had left to live for was this old farm."

Marlene's heart broke for him. Bill Walker had been kind to her, and he deserved better from the country he'd fought to protect. She pulled out her phone again and called.

"Tommy here."

"Tommy, it's Marlene. I need a favor."

"Name it and it's yours, Miss Marlene. How can I help?"

"I need everything you can get me about a man named Paul Hardy. I know he lives in this state and has an office of sorts in a town called Jonasville."

"Consider it done. I'll send it to your phone as soon as I get anything."

"Tommy, you're the best. Do you still have a tracking device on my car?"

"Of course."

"I'm sending a man north to you. He's human, but is aware of Vampires and has held his peace for a long time. He's a friend, Tommy. Bill's a country boy, when he nears the city you'll have to guide him. Set him up someplace outside the city where he can see the trees, and I'll take over when I get back. Access whatever funds you need from my accounts."

"Consider it done, ma'am. Who am I looking for?"

"The man's name is Bill Walker. Tommy, you're the best. Tell Olla she's lucky she saw you first." He was laughing with delight as she broke the connection.

Marlene turned to the two men. "All right, boys, you guys head north. I'll hang around here until I make Mr. Paul Hardy deceased." She saw the embarrassed look on Bill's face and her heart broke for him. "There's money in that secret compartment, Bill. Use it all if you have to."

He nodded shyly. "Why, girl? Why are you doing this?"

"Bill, I've lived a long time, several hundred years in fact, and in all that time I've rarely encountered the kindness you've shown me. I was the middle child of a brood of children, and as a child I slept in the barn with the animals.

"When we first met I'd spent the night in fresh sweet hay then was greeted warmly by a true gentleman. My grandfather always greeted me each morning just as you did. That whole experience gave me sweet memories.

"The kindness you showed me following that meeting cemented the friendship. I don't make many friends, Bill, and I cherish the ones I do. Please let me help you."

"All right, Marlene. I've got nowhere else to turn. I was planning to stay here and put up a fight, you know, go out in a blaze of glory. After all, I am dang near ninety years old."

She laughed at that then gave his shoulder a gentle squeeze. "There'll be none of that. I have a plan, and I need you to help me with it. Take Torvil and the car, head towards New York. There's a phone in the car. Answer if it rings, that should be Tommy. He'll help you."

He nodded and accepted the keys from her hand.

"That's all sweet and nice, girl, but I can't go with him," said Torvil.

Marlene turned to arch an eyebrow at him. "Why not?"

"I'm a wanted man, you said so yourself. I'm also rather distinctive of feature, easy to identify. If someone spots me in that car we'll both be in jail or dead before nightfall. Nothing personal, Bill, but your chances are better without me along."

Marlene sighed and let her shoulders sag. "He's right, Bill. You go on, we'll think of something else here." They watched him gather an old battered suitcase from the porch then get in the car and drive away.

As Bill disappeared from sight Marlene turned to Torvil. "We need a new plan."

"Easy money, girl. I can fool up the idiots who're hunting for me. I'll stay in this general area. Once you've done the deed we move on. We can travel through the forest until we get far enough north for your people to pick us up.

"All you have to do is wait here and Hardy will come to you tomorrow."

"Yeah? How do you figure that?"

"The bank foreclosed on this rundown old farm. As land it's pretty much worthless. The only reason I can see for them to play hardball with Bill is the land. It's probably in the path of the pipeline. If so, Hardy will be here tomorrow to make sure Bill is either gone, or dead."

"You're starting to scare me, Torvil."

"What? Surprised the caveman can actually think, reason something out?"

"Hey, back off, Mr. Over Sensitive. When did I ever..."

"Sorry, you're right, you didn't. I guess I've been living in the back hills too long. People around here are pretty quick to show their prejudices."

"Let's get into the shade before I perish. Torvil, the way you speak tells me you're a well educated man. Why are you living out here in the sticks?"

"Long story named Sweet Dorri. I'd be a lot happier in a castle setting down roots in a library. I had a large estate in Russia. My library was extensive, and I spent most of my time there. Bear hunting was forbidden on the estate, but I let the peasants hunt all the deer they wanted.

"I was content with my books and forest, but the Bolsheviks came through and burned the lot of it to the ground. I went bear and fled to the west, not stopping until I reached America."

Marlene smiled. "You and the king are going to get along just fine."

"Oh?"

"The king's a well read man as well. When he disappears he can always be found practicing with the sword, or in the library reading."

"Sounds like a man after my own heart," grinned Torvil. "Now, the sun's going down, I'll head into the trees."

"And I'll hide this truck in the barn. First thing in the morning I'll burn the place to the ground."

"Why?"

"So those bastards can't steal what Bill had to leave behind." Torvil nodded his approval, stepped out of his clothes then shimmered into the bear and ambled off into the trees.

High over head the hawk watched, wondering, "How does he do that?"

Scent of the Quarry

Once again Marlene slept in sweet smelling hay and dreamed of her childhood, a childhood that had been stolen all too soon. She'd been only sixteen when she was married off to a much older man, a man she'd hated. For five long years she'd endured that marriage from hell, and then the vampire came.

Like a maddened animal it had torn through the village, killing all before it. Marlene lay on the ground, bleeding, and near death, when she heard the battle roar of the great saber-toothed tiger. Before the vampire could finish her it was shredded by mighty claws, blood splashing over her face.

She'd choked on the blood then fainted. Much later she'd awakened, a terrible burning thirst driving her to near madness. She could smell blood, fresh blood. Drawn to that scent by a power she couldn't name, Marlene sought the source of that delightful scent. It was her husband, bleeding from a wound on his arm.

The force of her body slamming into him sent him sprawling with her atop him. Sharp fangs bit deep, and she moaned with delight as the hot sweet blood filled her mouth. She sucked greedily, but something was pulling at her, speaking to her, demanded an answer. What could it want that was so important at this moment?

"What's your name? Think, what's your name? Tell me, tell me your name."

Marlene pulled her fangs from the trembling man's neck and replied angrily. "Marlene, my name is Marlene."

"Good. Good. Focus on that. Tell me again, what is your name?"

Somehow that voice was cutting through the madness, helping her to remember. "Marlene, my name is Marlene. Why do you ask me this? Go away now, I need... so thirsty...need..."

"What is your name? Tell me your name."

She'd released her victim, still alive, and stood to face the tall woman who was so demanding of her name. "My name is Marlene, as I told you. Who are you? What do you want?"

"Marlene, think hard, do you know what has happened to you?"

"What? Of course I ... no, wait ... there was a demon, killing everyone. He hurt me, I fell, and ... yes, as I lay there another demon slew the first, it's blood nearly choked me, and I swooned. I awakened to a burning thirst. I... I bit my husband and drank his blood, I ... it slaked the thirst somewhat, but not enough. I need more ... I need to kill him. Lady, what has happened to me?"

"Come with me. I will explain, and I'll help you. Come."

"I must kill him first."

"No."

"I must. I was given to him to pay my father's debts. For many years he has hurt me. I'm strong now and he's weak. I want to kill him."

"So be it," said the tall woman. "Take him, drink of his blood until he's dead, and then we'll go far from this place. Remember your name, even as you drink, even as you kill, remember your name."

She did. Marlene drank the man dry and cast aside the body. The woman had asked her name twice and she had given the right answer each time. "Lady, what would happen if I forgot my name?"

"Then you would become the beast, even as that other one did. By focusing on your name, you remember who and what you truly are. If you forget then you become the beast, and I have to kill you.

"Come, Marlene, we will leave this place, and I'll teach you how to control the thirst, to overcome the beast within."

That was a lesson Marlene had never forgotten. In the days that followed she learned what she'd become, and she'd learned how to control it.

It had been as much a memory as a dream, and Marlene awakened with a smile. Those had been difficult days, but the mother tigress had been loving as well as stern. Marlene learned much, most of all a love of life and an ability to adapt to any situation.

She rose, stretched, then went into the house, found an empty box and started packing. She carefully wrapped pictures from the walls and a few trinkets that looked like they'd been special to the old man. In the end she filled two boxed and stored them in Bill's old truck.

Marlene drove off the property then parked and walked back. Just as she reached the house two cars came speeding up the drive. One was a police car.

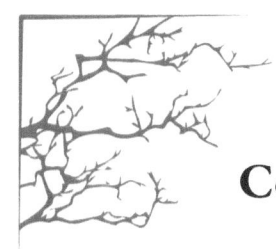

Contract Complete

The large man who climbed out of the fancy car was a bit of a dandy. "Fop," thought Marlene as she ran her gaze over him. The police car disgorged a sheriff and a deputy. Both men straightened their hats and swaggered towards her, guns drawn.

"Who are you?" demanded the sheriff.

"I'm Mary Jo Walker, Bill Walker's granddaughter. Who the hell are you, and what are you doing with those guns in your hands?"

"Shut up, woman, I ask the questions. Where is that old coot anyway?"

"He's gone. I got here last night, and he told me what happened. I assume you're here to evict an elderly war veteran from his home."

"I'm here to uphold the law and enforce a court ordered eviction. This property was seized by the bank and sold. The new owner wants it empty."

"I see."

"So where is that old bugger anyway?"

"Gramps was planning to shoot you, but I talked him into moving in with me. He took my car and went on ahead. I'll bring his truck and the last few boxes of his things. You're in luck, Sheriff, you live to bully people another day."

Marlene stepped past the two officers and faced the other man. "And you would be the new owner, am I right?"

"Right as rain, little girl," he leered as he reached for her.

She brushed away his hand and stepped closer. "Got a name, Mr. Property Owner?"

"I'm Paul Hardy. Now, what's your name, sweet cakes?"

51

"Already told you, I'm Mary Jo Walker. So why did you go to so much trouble to steal my grandfather's old farm?"

"I'm a land developer. This property has a world of potential," he smirked, still undressing her with his eyes.

She stepped even closer, reaching up until her nose actually brushed his cheek. She inhaled briefly then slapped his hand away and strode to Bill's old truck. "Smells like bullshit to me," she said, as she got in and started the engine. She drove away leaving the three men behind wondering what had just happened.

They inspected the house and found it empty then headed for the barn. They were halfway there when there was an explosion. The building instantly went up in flames.

While the men called for assistance, Marlene shipped the boxes of Bill's belongings to herself in New York, and then checked into a local motel. She was soaking away the weeks of dirt while men fought the fire. She smiled to herself as she relaxed in the bath. She had Paul Hardy's scent, now to get him alone.

It was evening when the men arrived at the bar, tired, dirty, and thirsty. The sheriff, deputy, and Paul Hardy were joined by two others and another group pulled up another table. That fire had burned hot and had taken all day to defeat.

While they drank and bitched, a dark-haired woman at the bar smiled to herself. "Sounds like you boys had a bad day," she said in a sexy purr, as she pulled up a chair and sat beside Paul Hardy. His scent was hidden beneath the smell of the soot, but she smiled as she easily recognized it.

"Indeed we have, little lady," he said, as he laid his hand on the well tanned brunette's knee.

"Looks like you've been fighting fire. That's thirsty work."

"Yes we were. After a day like this a man needs a beer and a bit of recreation, if you get what I mean." His hand slid up her thigh as he spoke.

She stood and smiled wickedly. "Maybe so, but I'd suggest a bath first." She patted his shoulder then walked towards the door. "I'll come back near closing time for a night cap," she said as she reached the exit.

She could hear the men laughing and making cat calls and lewd suggestions as she allowed the door to swing shut behind her. Grinning, Marlene returned to her motel and relaxed to wait for night to fall.

At an hour before closing time, a freshly scrubbed Paul Hardy, without his wedding ring, returned to the bar. There was no sign of the dazzling brunette. He was angry at being played for a fool when the bar closed. He stormed out and got into his car.

As Paul Hardy started the engine he felt another presence with him. A glance in the mirror revealed the dark-haired beauty. "Well it's about time you came back, Sugar. Now, drive someplace where we can be alone for a while."

With a leer he pulled the car into gear and drove away. A short drive later he parked at a lookout. There was a fine view of the town and deep forest behind, Marlene was pleased. This was perfect and she had easy access to an escape route.

"So, sweet cakes, are you coming up here with me, or am I going back there with you?"

"Why don't we take a stroll under the stars. I've always liked sex under the open sky the best."

"Works for me," he replied, as he opened the car door and got out. He reached to open the door for her, but instead of the dark-haired woman he expected to find, he found a monster. Paul Hardy staggered back as the half cat/half woman leaped from the car.

The demon's voice froze him in his tracks. *"Stand still, make no sound until I command it."* Swallowing hard, he none the less froze in place, quaking with fear.

She smiled as she approached him, her long fangs gleaming in the moonlight. *"Tell me truthfully, did you rape and kill Doris Martin?"*

"Yes."

"Take out your cell phone and record a full confession of the event, express remorse, then shut off the phone."

Trembling in fear and fighting it all the way, he none the less pulled out the phone. He was unable to resist the compulsion of that voice. She stepped back from him as he began to speak. "A couple of months ago me and the boys paid a visit to the widow Martin. She was playing hardball and I needed that property. The nasty old nigger said the wrong thing and I lost it.

"I knocked her down, tore off her clothes, and gave her what she deserved. When I was done the boys all took a turn, but she was still fighting us. I kicked her and kept it up until they joined in and she eventually stopped breathing. What I did there was wrong, and I hate myself for it." Trembling, he shut off the phone then dropped it on the ground.

The demon inspected the phone to make certain it was shut off, then rose to face him. Suddenly she leaped at him, those needle sharp fangs bit deep and she moaned with pleasure as the blood spurted into her waiting mouth. She drank deeply for a moment then pushed him away. *"You may now move and speak."*

He staggered then fell backward. "What the hell are you?"

"Vampire," she purred seductively. "You know, you're a nasty piece of work, sir."

"What are you going to do to me?"

"I'm going to kill you. Paul Hardy, for your crime against Doris Martin, you will now forfeit your miserable life." He screamed in terror as she leaped at him, her razor sharp claws slashing. She ripped and tore at him until he lay still, the last vestiges of his life's blood draining out onto the hard packed dirt.

Marlene shimmered back into the woman and tore her dress off, placing the torn garment in his dead hand. She stepped out of her shoes then returned to the car and retrieved her backpack from the back seat.

Naked, she fled into the forest. Once she found a small stream she stepped into it and walked away. The moonlight soon showed her some bare rock and she stepped out onto it, quickly dressed in her hiking clothes and started out.

It took her two days to reach Bill Walker's old farm again, the hawk following her all the way. When she arrived there was police tape around the place, but there was no sign of humans. Slowly, carefully, she began to cast about for a familiar scent. A while later a faint trace teased her nose. The bear had been here recently.

The next morning Torvil awakened to find Marlene resting under a tree near him. "Well?" he asked.

"Mission accomplished," she replied. "Paul Hardy is dead. Before he died he made a full confession of his murder of Doris Martin and recorded it on his phone. It will be discovered when they find his body."

"Now that's the best news I've had in a while. How did he die?"

"From the looks of it he was torn apart by a bear," she grinned.

Torvill sighed deeply and leaned back against a tree. "Then it's done. I can let my sweet Dorrie rest now. All right, girl, you kept your end of the bargain."

"We're not quite finished yet. When I complete an assignment I always provide irrefutable evidence of the kill. Usually the head, but in this case, a newscast from the Internet will suffice. Take a look."

She passed him her phone and he read the account of Hardy's body being found, and the confession that was found on his phone. The hunt for the bear has been intensified. Torvil nodded his head and passed back the phone. "Well done, girl. All right, what's the next move. I promised to behave and talk to your king, and I will. You're the boss, what do we do now?"

"Well, as you pointed out the other day, we should keep you out of the public eye. We'll keep to the trees until we can make contact with the king's people. We'll head north until we can get picked up."

"Works for me, but can you keep yourself fed in the forest? I don't want to wake up one day with a hungry vampire chewing on my ass." Her hearty laughter brought a wide grin to his face.

WHILE MARLENE WAS REPORTING to Torvil of her successful assassination, others were at the site of the murder. The deputy sheriff sighed as he watched the tall man talking to the small wiry fellow who kept staring at the ground. Finally the small man got down and sniffed at the ground. He stood and turned to the taller man. "Wan't a bear, suh. Somethin' else."

"Something else, what else could have done this?"

"Don' know. Never scent that before. Dangerous, vengeful, though."

"Whatever the hell it was, find it, kill it." The small man nodded, pulled a rifle from the back of the truck, slung it over his shoulder then set out into the trees.

As he disappeared from sight the deputy spoke. "Harlan, what the hell was all that about?"

"Someone or something killed my brother, and I want it dead. That fella is from the back bayou country. Strange as hell, but they say he can follow a trail through water. They also say he's part cottonmouth and part bloodhound. Once he takes the trail, whatever he's tracking is already dead."

"Right."

"I saw him fight once, a big hard man, but the little snake brought him down. I never seen anything that fast or half as savage before. He hunts, kills, and eats his food raw. You notice he didn't take anything with him except the rifle."

"So you hired him to find Paul's killer."

"Damn right I did. Must be over a hundred men trying to hunt down that damned bear and they've all come up empty, if they survived. Soon as I heard about Paul I called and hired LeBlanc. He'll find it, kill it, and bring me its head. Let's go, we're done here."

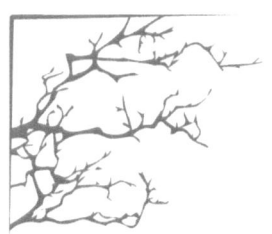

Castle

They'd spent much of the day exploring the property, and the more he saw the more pleased the king became. The house was massive, a true mansion or manor house. There were many separate living quarters, as the old fellow had created it to house a small army of security people. The entrance was fenced, gated, and there was indeed a moat. A small stream had been diverted and dammed for that purpose.

The moat served another purpose as well. Just beyond the house, where the stream returned to its natural path, there was a small generation plant. The place was completely off grid. The lawns were huge and well kept up, and the house was spotless, even though no one lived there anymore.

For Harald, the huge library was a bonus, as was the warren of underground rooms and passageways. There were also offices and a large meeting room, a billiard room, and a spacious and well-equipped exercise room. Three of the underground passageways led into the forest.

Behind the house was a swimming pool, tennis court, more lawns, a hangar that could easily accommodate the plane and a runway that could handle another small plane. More than enough room to land the jet. Once into the forest the land began to rise until it was rugged mountains and steep cliffs.

"Well, Sire, what do you think? Will it meet your needs?" asked Amanda as they finished the tour in the meeting room.

"Personally, I like it," he replied. "However, I want honest assessments from all of you. Amanda, can you and Clyde function optimally here?"

"Easily, Sire. I do have some disturbing memories of life here, but Clyde can help me through them. I vote yes."

"Gudrun?"

"I like it," she replied. "It's hard to reach, easy to defend, and there are bolt holes if it must be abandoned. However, I'd like to find forest paths from the escape tunnels to more populated areas where transportation and food could be acquired."

"Georg?"

"I like it, Sire. The Children of the Wolf could thrive here. We can reach the forest unseen and return the same way. We could find those paths for Miss Gudrun easily."

"Eric?"

"I like it, Sire. It reminds me of home, the plane can land easily, and we have a place to hide it. However, there is a problem, isn't there, Gudrun."

"Yes, Eric, there are two major issues, as I'm sure the king is aware."

"Staff and a cover story to account for all the food and supplies coming and going from the place," sighed Harald.

"The cover story is easy," said Amanda. "Grandfather was known to house a large security force here. The sight of Eric or Jimmy in uniform at the gate house or in town would reinforce that idea. I'm sure we can find a few discrete people to staff the place. You could put them under compulsion if necessary."

"How much staff do we actually need?" asked Sally. "Can't we look after ourselves as we are now?"

"Much of the food our people need could be produced on the farmland between us and the highway," mused Harald. "The vampires would have to travel to the city to hunt, of course.

"Sally, my beloved, I fear we will need staff, at least a dozen."

"Harald?"

"We'll need a couple of men as groundskeepers, three kitchen staff, and a few cleaners."

Sally gently took his face in her hands and smiled as she gazed into his eyes. "My beloved husband, you have made me a queen, but I wasn't born to privilege. I can cook my own food and keep my living space clean."

Harald smiled and kissed her fingers. "I know you can, my sweet, but you're the queen now and shouldn't have to. No, we'll have to do this the old-fashioned way."

"The old-fashioned way?"

"Live in servants, my love," sighed the king. "They live in the house with us and basically become part of the family."

"Part of the family?"

"We mark them, my queen," said Gudrun. "Just as Gina did with Marco, we mark them to ensure their silence and loyalty. A century ago we all kept a few devoted servants. We marked them and used the compulsion on them as well. We made sure they had good lives, kept them safe, and allowed them to retire in comfort."

"Enslave them?"

"Is your life so bad, my sweet?"

"Harald, no, that's not what I meant, and you know it. You love me too, but if you didn't..."

"It's not quite like that, Sally, my love. We do love them too, but not as strongly as I do you, as Gudrun loves Terry, or Ella loves Kylie."

Sally sat back and sighed. "It's more like Gina and Marco, right? He's utterly devoted to her, and she treats him like a spoiled puppy. They're more like pets?"

"Yes, that's a much closer description than slave. We choose them carefully and are careful to never abuse them, see they have good lives."

Sally still didn't look impressed. "I have to tell you; I don't like being seen as a lesser species."

"Sally, that isn't how we see you and you know it. When have I, or any of the others, treated you like a lesser being?"

"He's right, my queen," smiled Gudrun. "Since you've been queen you've grown as a person, and as a leader, as well as providing an anchor and support to our king. I have obeyed your every command to the best of my ability, and never once felt inferior. Neither do I feel superior to you.

"My queen, there are people who are born with a desire to serve, to be protected, provided for, and to serve the provider."

"You mean like some of the people who practice BDSM?"

"Yes," said Amanda, "I believe that is exactly what Gudrun is saying. Am I right? Are these the people you choose?"

"Yes," Harald replied, "this is the type of person we choose. Yes, Gina took Marco by force, but that was under different circumstances. With these people a bargain is struck, they're marked, and so it goes."

Somewhat placated, Sally relaxed her defensive posture. "So, just how will you find these people? Are you planning to join a BDSM club?"

"That will be up to me and Clyde," replied Amanda, a rare smile playing at her lips. "Clyde and I will interview them and be certain before they're hired and marked."

At this point Eric took pity on the king. "Sire, I get the impression you have something more in mind for this place than just the court as it is now."

"Very astute, Eric," grinned Harald, grateful for the change of subject. "Yes, things are getting out of hand, especially in the city. First all we had to do was keep the vampires out of the public eye. That was difficult enough, but then we learned of the Children of the Wolf. They needed our help, and as fellow non-humans, and to protect our own anonymity, we joined with them. Now Marlene is bringing us a were-bear.

"The point is, we could find ourselves with dozens of different kinds of non-humans, and, like it or not, it seems to be falling to us to protect them. We need a place of sanctuary for them."

"And a place to confine those who are just too different?"

"Yes, Eric. That as well, for those who cannot conform, we must confine and protect or kill. Killing will be a last resort."

"With that vision, Sire, I believe this place to be a far superior base than the warehouses in the city," said Gudrun.

"So, we are agreed then?" There were nods all round. "Sally my love, before we commit to this, and the vision for it, will you do a reading for us. We have all come to trust your insights."

She nodded then began a series of deep breaths as she released herself to her special vision. No one spoke to disturb her, and it was a long time before she roused from the trance like state. "What did you see, my love?"

"Most of it is unclear, and a lot is somewhat disturbing. There is an air of unreasoning fear about this place, but we can change that energy, and I believe we should. I see this place becoming a refuge of peace, like the eye of the storm, but I see the rest of the country falling under a dark cloud. Already I see people poking into the affairs of the New York base.

"Our people have that under control at the moment, but it's only a matter of time. Harald, we do need a safer place, and this looks like the best bet."

"But?"

"The country is coming apart at the seams, my love. I think we should also develop a plan B."

The king sighed heavily again. Finally he raised his head and spoke. "Gudrun, you say you have knowledge of places in Europe that would suit our needs."

"Yes, Sire. One is a bolt hole we have used before. It's an abandoned Soviet military base. It's a bit more austere than this, but it has far better facilities for confining any non-humans we might need to keep away from others. Also, there is that castle of yours in Germany. Might it not do?"

"Yes it would, Gudrun, and it was my first choice, but with all the Americans we have with us it would be hard to explain away. All right, we move here as quickly as possible. As soon as we're settled in, you take Eric and the lads to Europe and find us a backup sanctuary."

Harald pulled out his phone and dialed.

"Tommy here, Sire."

"Tommy, tell everyone to start packing up. As soon as possible we're moving out."

"Yes Sir, and none too soon."

"Oh?"

"Miss Ella and Peter captured a couple of undercover cops snooping around. They put the fix on them, but..."

"Understood. Any word from Marlene?"

"She's neutralized the target and is returning, but it'll take a bit of time. Since Torvil is a wanted man, and has somewhat distinctive features, they're returning overland through the forest. She'll stay in touch as much as possible until we can pick them up."

"Very good, Tommy. Start the process in motion and we'll be back as soon as possible." Harald dropped the phone into his pocket and stood. "As soon as we're settled in here I intend to spend a week in that library." Sally smiled and patted his hand.

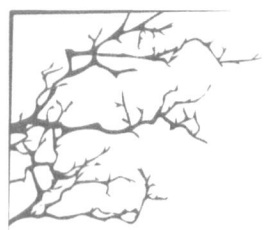

Hunted

Marlene wasn't having a great day. They'd barely left the farmyard when the sheriff arrived with three other truckloads of hunters. His voice had carried well, and Marlene had heard him.

"Now, you men are all hunter/trackers. We know that damned bear is still in the area, and now it's killed Paul Hardy. The dogs tracked it until they lost the scent, but it was headed north. We'll start from here. This is a killer bear. Take no chances, but make that thing dead.

"Oh, and for Christ's sake, if you see that crazy hunter Harlan hired, get the hell away from him. That man ain't right in the head."

There followed the sound of baying hounds; Marlene started swearing. If they'd followed a scent from Paul Hardy's corpse then it was her scent they were following. She rushed ahead and caught up to the bear. "It's hunters, a dozen or more. They're tracking me. You keep heading north, I'll catch up."

The bear grunted and gave her a friendly nudge then set out again. Marlene sat down and rubbed herself around on the ground then stood and went west.

"What is it? What the hell is going on here?"

"Stay back, Sheriff, so I can read the tracks here. Shit, this don't make no sense at all."

"What?"

"They were here, looks like a woman in hiking boots and the bear. The bear went north, and she went west. Thing is, the dogs want to go west."

"Well crap. There was a woman with Paul when he was killed, but she was in heels, and we found a piece of her dress in his hand. I don't

64

know who or what was here, but if the scent the dogs are on goes west, then we go west. Whoever or whatever that is, I have questions, and that woman will have the answers."

"Sheriff?"

"It's startin' to look like that's a tame bear, or at least a trained bear. I want to know who's givin' it the kill order, and why. We go after the woman. If we see the bear, kill it, but I want the woman alive."

The man nodded then set the dogs on Marlene's trail again. It wasn't going to be any fun at all. She headed west and into the roughest terrain she could find. Running in full vampire mode, she easily climbed trees, leaped swampy areas, and scaled rock faces that tormented the men on her trail.

Several times the dogs stopped in confusion, blocked by terrain they could not overcome. Where she scaled the rocks, they had to find ways around, swampy areas had to be circled, and the scent relocated. Eventually they stopped and camped for the night. She didn't.

A vampire on the hunt can go for many days without food or rest, and this was the same. Steadily, Marlene led them into denser and rougher areas. When they camped on the third night they were exhausted.

The vampire was tired as well, but she was also hungry. While they slept soundly she circled back, creeping up on their camp.

The overtired men slept too soundly and didn't hear the dogs whimpering in fear. The hounds sensed a predator was near, and they cringed closer together. Terrified they watched as something slipped into the camp and seized a sleeping man, then dragged him silently into the trees.

He struggled wildly at first, but as the sting of her fangs numbed his muscles, he began to relax in her arms. Not daring to take too much she thrust him away. *"You were sleepwalking. You saw nothing."* With that she was gone into the darkness.

Unseen by the man or the vampire, cold slitted eyes had watched from hiding. "So, a blood drinker. Very dangerous, Cher. Very dangerous."

As the light of day returned to the forest, the hunter staggered back into camp. "Where the hell were you?"

"Must have been sleepwalking," he muttered. "Didn't see a damn thing."

"Yeah, well, grab a bite and get a move on. Looks like the dogs caught the scent again." This time the dogs turned north.

MARLENE WAS WELL AHEAD of the hunters when the daylight failed. The one she'd fed off had struggled to keep up, and that had held them back a bit. As well, the dogs didn't seem to be in as much of a hurry to catch up either. They spent a lot of time being wary and huddling close together.

As Marlene rested high on a ledge the hunters wouldn't be able to reach, she sighed and wondered how Torvil was doing. She was growing uneasy, as though something unseen was following her. And then there was the damned hawk. It was perched high on a rocky crag, watching her.

Long before dawn, her night vision allowed her to descend from the ledge. As she reached the ground she saw a skunk on the trail. With a wicked grin she tensed then moved. With lightning speed she swept down on the poor creature, kicked dirt in its face then streaked away before the deadly mist could reach her.

"There now, that should give those hounds something to think about." She was grinning as she headed into a swamp, still going north. Two days later she crossed the bear's trail. She smelled the blood.

It was near dark the next day when she found him, holed up in a small cave. He was in bad shape and refused to change to human form. "You heal faster as the bear?" The response was a gentle grunt. "I'll go hunting."

An hour later the vampire returned to the cave with the body of a small deer. The bear was weak so she tore chunks of meat from the carcass and fed it to him. When he could eat no more she went back outside to watch through the night.

Nothing disturbed the bear's rest and in the morning he awakened stronger. He was finishing off the last of the meat as she returned. "Feeling better?" she asked. A soft grunt and a lick for her hand was the response. "Still need to stay in bear form I see. All right, I'll go hunting again. I'll see if I can bring you water also."

She was true to her word. Before noon she had brought another small deer and used a piece of the hide from the first one to carry water for him. She held it carefully while he lapped it up then sighed.

"All right, my furry friend, the sun's high and it's getting hot. I've been days without rest, so I'm going to settle down in this nice cool cave for a long nap. I need you to stay awake. If you hear, smell, or see anything you don't like, wake me and I'll deal with it. Understand?"

He grunted and licked her hand again. Marlene settled down and was instantly asleep. Normally, when on a hunt like this she would catch a few naps during the heat of the day and dark of the night. However, first she had shaken off the hunters, then trailed and found Torvil, and then stayed awake to watch for three days while the bear healed. Marlene was exhausted. She was also uneasy, whatever was following her had come much closer while the bear recovered.

She fell asleep just before noon and it was near dawn again before she awakened. Awakened and was thirsty for blood. The bear was gone from the cave. She bolted from the cave to find him in human form, sitting on a boulder, keeping watch.

For a moment they locked eyes. Finally he grinned. "Awake, at last I see."

"Obviously."

"You're hungry, you need to feed. There's a small cluster of cabins beside a lake about three miles that way." He pointed south east. She leaped away so fast she fairly disappeared before his eyes. He chuckled and settled down to wait for her to return. Even as he seemingly relaxed he was watchful, wary. Something was out there, stalking them. Every instinct he had was telling him to run.

She was like a ghost, moving silently through the trees, even as the hawk soared overhead. Before long she caught the scent of blood as well as other farm smells. She moved in, slowly circling the small farm. She found him in the barn.

The farmer had just slaughtered a hog. It was hanging up and the blood was being collected in a bucket set beneath it. The man looked up, startled then tried to scream, but powerful fingers seized his throat choking off any sound.

Marlene was nearly mad with the burning thirst for blood as she looked into the open door of the barn. She instantly attacked. He saw her coming, but wasn't fast enough to react. Strong fingers grabbed his throat and needle sharp fangs bit deep. She moaned with delight and drank greedily for a long moment.

Fighting herself all the way, she finally thrust him away. Wide eyed, he staggered and fell, watching in horror as she seized up the pail of blood from beneath the pig and drank greedily. He was still sitting on the floor, fingering his knife as she stopped and dropped the pail onto the floor and kicked it aside.

The nightmare facing him looked like a hard muscled woman, but her fingers ended in sharp claws and her leonine face had long fangs as well cat's whiskers. When she spoke her voice was that of a demon from hell.

"Obey me. You are not feeling well. You accidentally kicked over the pail and spilled all the pig's blood. I was never here. You did not see anything unusual in the barn." With that she turned and raced from the barn.

Bewildered, the man picked himself up off the barn floor. "Well, shit. Spilled the works of it. Goddamn it anyway." Slowly, painfully, he went back to work.

"So, you've had your fill, blood drinker. You'll be stronger now. We wait, Cher, we wait for the right time." The mad eyed hunter retreated deeper into the forest. "I see you up there, wind rider. Beware LeBlanc don' decide to eat you too."

It was nearly noon when Marlene returned to the cave. "Feeling better?" chuckled Torvil.

"Much," she replied, as she shimmered back to the young woman for the first time in many days. "It's too damned hot out here, let's wait in the cave until it cools off a bit."

"Works for me," he replied, rising and following her back inside. They settled down in the cool shade then he spoke again. "Marlene, thank you. I owe you my life in more ways than one. Don't get me wrong here, but I don't understand."

"What is it you don't understand, Torvil?"

"Why you're doing this for me."

"King's orders. Just doing my job."

"Oh horse feathers."

That made her laugh and he grinned with delight to hear it. "Horse feathers? Don't tell me, that was one of your wife's sayings, right?"

"Yes, it was. I used to tell her that I could remember a time when horses did indeed have feathers." That made her chuckle again. "So, will you tell me why? I'm no fool, girl, and I've lived under the rule of a good many kings. I'll bet you had orders to bring me back or kill me, and I'll also wager you have the power to make that judgment yourself."

Marlene sighed deeply and leaned back against the stone wall of the cave. She really needed more rest. "All right, Torvil. Yes, I do have the right to make the final decision. I'll also confess, it would normally have been an easy decision to make."

"But?"

"You're unique, my furry friend. In all the world you're the only caveman or bear I've ever known in all my long life. More, it was the reason you were killing those men. Through all the centuries I've never been loved as deeply as you loved your Doris, except once centuries ago. That alone told me you were worthy of keeping alive.

"Moreover, you've managed to survive for fifty thousand years or more, I wasn't about to be the one to end that. Also, you are, without doubt, one of the most intelligent men I have ever met. Last, but not least, you make me laugh. You can't begin to understand what that means to me."

"Tell me," he said, as he sank to the ground with his back to the wall.

"As a child I laughed often. I was part of a large family, and we had a good life. That ended when I was sixteen and given in marriage to a cruel man. For five long years I endured until I was made vampire."

"How did that happen?"

"Just as you're unique in all the world, my friend, so am I. I'm the only living vampire, besides the great mother, who was made this way completely by accident. All the others asked for, begged for, the change."

"But not you?"

"No. Mother, the only one of us who can fully become the saber-toothed tiger, she who was first, will hunt and kill any vampire who can't control the killing lust. It was she who made an end of Mobutu.

"One vampire she had made went on a mad killing spree. She tracked him across France until she cornered him in my village. He had already slaughtered most of the people and was tearing me apart, drinking my blood, when she attacked. I was still alive, barely, and his blood spilled onto my face. I swallowed by reaction.

"I awakened many hours later, healed in body, but with a burning thirst, a madness that only the blood of a living human could slake. I found the husband who had abused me and attacked. She discovered me there and helped me break through the madness. She taught me how to control it, and here I am.

"So you see, Torvil my friend, you and I are unique and need to watch each other's back."

He chuckled at that, and, with a soft smile, rose to his feet. "Get some sleep, little sister. I'll keep watch."

"Torvil, watch carefully."

"I know, I feel it too. Something's out there, hunting us, and it's not human, or friendly."

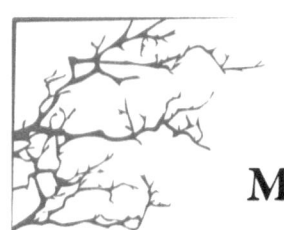

Moving the Court

Bill Walker had driven north for most of the day. It was getting late when he heard the phone ring. Pulling off the road, he answered. "Marlene's car, Bill Walker here."

"Mr. Walker, my name's Tommy. Marlene asked me to help you until she returns. Do you have sufficient funds, Sir."

"I've got a few dollars, why?"

"Things are a bit lively here at the moment. Would you consider taking a hotel for the night then we can get together tomorrow and decide how to proceed from there?"

"Sure, works for me."

"Cool. Here's a number to call if you suddenly need anything. It'll reach me any time day or night." Tommy gave him the number and he wrote it down then pulled back onto the road.

Bill knew he was nearing New York city, but he had long since abandoned the highways for secondary roads. He found a small town and took a motel room for the night. After a meal at the cafe, he settled back with the remote and started flicking channels. It did no good and he gave it up.

"So what the hell have I gotten myself into this time?" he mused. "Goddamn banks anyway." He'd needed the money for a new well, and he hadn't had it. He was in his late sixties when he took out the loan and had to put the property up as collateral. He'd never managed to pay it off. That bastard Paul Hardy had bought up the loan and called it.

"Dirty bastard, I hope she does kill him. Ah well, it's all done now. The little girl seems to have a plan, and she swore she'd never harm me, so I'll trust that. Hurts to become a charity case though. Wonder what

72

the plan is? She seemed to know that guy I saw in Germany, wonder if I'll get to see him again?"

He continued his musings until he fell asleep. He arose early the next morning as all farmers do, bought breakfast at the cafe, and then set out slowly towards the city that never sleeps. It wasn't long before the phone rang. He pulled over to answer. "Tommy?"

"Yes sir, good morning, did you sleep well?"

"I did indeed."

"All right, now, I'm ready to get things on the go. There's a small town a few miles from where you are. Just keep going then find a cafe, I'll meet you there."

"A few miles? Boy, it'll take you hours to get out of that monster you call a city."

Tommy laughed at that. "Not to worry, Mr. Walker, I've been on the road for quite a while. We're already outside the city. Just find a cafe and order us a coffee."

"Us? How many of you are there?"

"Two, my wife is with me."

"All right, coffee it is." Bill hung up and set out again. About fifteen minutes later he came upon a small town, found the local cafe and settled in. He ordered three coffees and said folks were joining him there. The cups had barely arrived when a tall lanky man and a woman entered. The man looked like a typical office geek, as Bill called them, but the woman was athletic looking.

Spotting him, she approached and spoke with a strong Slavic accent. "You are Mr. Bill Walker, yes?"

"Yes, ma'am."

"I'm Olla, and this shy fellow is my Tommy." They slid into the booth with him and mixed the coffee.

"Still hot, not bad," grinned Tommy. "So, Mr. Walker, did Marlene give you any idea at all what she has in mind for you?"

"Bill. Call me Bill. No, Tommy, she didn't. It all happened pretty quick. She hid her car in the barn then lit out. When she got back I was being foreclosed on and kicked off the property. Long story short, she sent me to you and took a different path home."

The old man turned his attention to Olla. "You're like Marlene, but different."

"I'm Russian," she replied, with a twinkle in her eye.

"Ah, so that's it." Bill grinned and nodded his head knowingly.

"Yes, Marlene is French."

"I'm old, girl, it's hard for me to keep it straight sometimes. Now, Tommy, he's American like me, right?"

"Exactly," she grinned in reply. "We are all different, but the same."

Tommy started to speak, but his phone rang. He excused himself and stepped outside to answer. "Tommy here."

"Tommy, start packing, we're moving the court to new quarters. Contact Ilya and inform him. Has there been any word from Marlene?"

"Yes, Sire, she reported in, but there's a problem. She's bringing the were-bear overland through the forest. She's also sent a man to us for protection. He's human but aware of what she is. I was going to put him in a hotel until she gets back, but I don't think this is a good idea."

"Oh?"

"He's not under any compulsion and he knew instantly that Olla wasn't completely human."

"Bring him to the court, Tommy. I want to talk to this man."

"As you command, Sire." Tommy put the phone back in his pocket and returned.

"Tommy?"

"Olla my love, we have a problem here. Things have just gone sideways, as usual. Mr. Walker, my employer, Mr. Eldredsson would like to meet you. He's asked me to bring you to the office."

"There's only one problem with that. I hate driving in the city. I'll get lost long before we get there."

Olla chuckled at that. "You ride with Tommy, Mr. Bill. I will bring Marlene's car back home. I know the way."

Bill sat watching out the window as Tommy drove through the city that seemed to go on forever. Tommy had spent much of the time on the phone that was plugged into his ear. Finally he turned his attention to the old man. "Ever been to New York before, Bill?"

"Nope. Even small towns give me the willies, this is something else again. So, Olla your wife?"

"Indeed she is."

"Pretty girl, not vampire like Marlene, but something else."

"Olla is a were-wolf, Bill. How could you tell she's different?"

"Couldn't say for sure. Just something about the eyes, the way she moves, something almost feral, yet not."

"Well I'll be damned. You know, I've never met anyone else who could tell."

"I'm not surprised," grinned the old fellow as he turned his attention to Tommy, "most folks can't, I expect." Before Tommy could respond there was a blare of a horn and a loud voice swearing.

Olla smiled and waved at the angry man then snuggled the car up close to Tommy's. "She's having way too much fun with that guy," sighed Tommy, as he crawled through the traffic light. "We'll be home in a few minutes. With any luck the king will be back and can see you."

"The king? What does he want with me?"

"He'll want to ask you about Marlene and her mission."

"He'll also want to know how much I know about other things, and if I can't give the right answers he'll make me disappear."

"No, I didn't say ..."

"You didn't have to, Tommy boy. I can read between the lines."

"We're here and there's the bus. The king's home."

Bill watched in silence as the car disappeared inside a warehouse, Olla close behind. Tommy led him into a large office area. He was gazing all around when a big man with golden hair breezed through.

He waved his hand and Olla took Bill's arm then followed the big fellow.

"Tommy, see if you can locate Marlene. Mr. Walker, sit here." The king pulled out a chair for him then sat near it. A woman joined them and took the big man's hand. Nervously, Bill sat. "So, Mr. Walker, Marlene sent you to us. Did she say why?"

"Bill, call me Bill. You would be the king she works for. No sir, she didn't say."

"Sire, if I may..."

"Go ahead, Tommy."

"Sir, Marlene said that Bill's a friend, that he's been forced off his land, and she asked me to look out for him until she can get back. She said Bill is aware of vampires, but hasn't ever said anything about that. I thought you would want to speak to him yourself. Sire, Bill instantly recognized that Olla is different too."

"Indeed. You made the right call, Tommy. Bill, relax, nobody here is going to hurt you. Marlene would skin us alive if we did." He was grinning and Bill started to relax.

The woman beside him smiled and reached for his hand. "Hi Bill, I'm Sally."

"A pleasure, ma'am. I can see you're human, but with a slight difference as well."

"I'm psychic, Bill. I suspect you have a touch of the talent too."

Harald leaned his elbows on the table and smiled reassuringly as he spoke. "Bill, you've known of the existence of vampires but didn't speak of it to anyone?"

"That's right. First time I saw one was in Germany back in '44. I was sixteen, lied like hell to get in the army, and was sent over at the end of the war. I saw a big Russian go down under a hail of gunfire, but a few minutes later he got back up, grabbed a German soldier, bit his neck then tossed the body aside. Marlene said his name was likely Peter."

"Yes, probably."

"That fella, Torvil, Marlene had with her, he's something else again."

"What do you mean?"

"Marlene's like you, Olla is different, but not human, Torvil is something else again. Not like either of you, different from Olla, but still not entirely human."

"That's quite a talent you have there, Mr. Walker," said the king, relaxing back in his chair. "Tell me, why did you never speak of this to anyone?"

Bill grinned as well. "What, and get locked up, filled with drugs, shock treatments? Oh hell no. I kept my mouth shut, my head down, and my eyes open. The plan was simple, if I saw one, run like hell and hide."

"Did you ever see any others?"

"A few over the years, but not up close until the little gal showed up in the barn. I knew what she was, but had nowhere to run. She offered me no harm and needed help, so I took a chance."

"I'm curious, Bill," said Sally. "Knowing what she was, why would you help her?"

He sighed and let his shoulders slump. "I'm old, Sally. In my long life I've watched my fellow humans just get meaner and meaner to each other. I knew what would likely happen if she was found out, so I helped her.

"You see, when the big Russian bit the German, the German got up and walked away a few minutes later. I took a chance I could survive an encounter with the girl, but I knew if I talked everybody else would just start shooting.

"I thought she'd head back to the city, but she showed up again a couple of days later. She caught on that I knew what she was, promised she would never hurt me because we're friends, and I believed her. When she found out I'd been forced off my land, she got pretty mad about it, then she called Tommy. The rest you know."

The king sat lost in thought for a moment then spoke. "Have you always been a farmer, Bill?"

"Yep, lived on the land for most of my eighty odd years. I don't know any other kind of life. Don't really want to." He sighed and his shoulders sagged. "Guess I'd better learn to adapt. So, you going to kill me?"

"Kill you? No, I'm going to put you to work, if you're willing."

"A job? At my age? Oh hell, why not, ... is there a pension plan?" Sally's sweet laughter brought another grin to his face. "So, what have you got for me? Bear in mind now, I'm old. There's barely enough blood in these old veins to keep me going, I won't make much of a food source."

The king's great roar of laughter brought a smile to the old man's face. "Actually, I was hoping you'd agree to help me feed my human allies. I need a farmer.

"Allow me to explain. We're moving the lot of us to a more defensible spot. The political situation in this country is going to hell in a hurry. Anybody who's the least bit different will soon become a target, and we're far too exposed here.

"We have a new home to go to, somewhat out of the cities, and far more defensible. Between the new royal castle and the highway there are a couple of small farms, one abandoned and the other up for sale.

"Bill, I'd like to install you on one of those farms, to produce a source of food for the humans among us, and as a buffer against prying eyes. With your talent, you could easily tell if something wasn't quite right and could warn us. We'll provide the farm and anything else you might need. We'll also take care of all your financial needs."

"That all sounds right sweet and all, but I'm dang near ninety years old. I don't expect to last a lot longer. You might want to take that into consideration."

"Marlene says you're a friend, Bill. We take care of our friends. Don't worry, there'll be strong young men to help with the hard labor. Come on, what say you, be our lookout?"

"You folks are all crazy, you know that? In all honesty, it would be easier for you, and a lot safer, to just put me down."

"Harald told you," smiled Sally, "we take care of our friends. Come on, what have you got to lose?"

"Not a dang thing," he replied, a small catch in his voice. "I'll take the job."

"Done then," said Harald as he offered his hand. "Tommy, where are we with the move?"

"The trucks are being loaded as we speak, Sire."

"Illya's people?"

"Eric just left with the bus, Sire."

"Excellent, Tommy. I get the sense Bill here isn't a man of the cities, a country boy, as you Americans say. Perhaps you could ..."

"Already arranged, Sire," grinned Tommy. "Vasily is driving one of the trucks. Bill can ride with him, and Amanda can set him up in the castle until the farms are ready."

"Efficient as always, Tommy. Well done."

"So, Bill, you said you've seen a few others over the years. Can you tell me what kind? Were they vampires, or something else?"

"Something else, usually. There's strange things that crawl out of the back bayou country, some in the hills too. Saw a kid once who had a lot of cottonmouth snake in him. Evil little bastard, he was. Kept well clear of him. There was another fella, wasn't too sure about him, either. He was real skittish, like a deer. Only got a glimpse of him then never saw him again."

"Anything recent?" asked the king.

"Nope, just the little gal and Torvil the bear, oh, and Olla this morning."

"All right, keep an eye open and let me know if you see anything. Tommy will take you to the truck now. We'll see you again in a couple of days."

Hot Days on the Trail

The day was hot, end of August hot, and Marlene could actually smell the heat. She muttered something about it while they dozed in the shade of an oak tree. Suddenly the bear raised his head and looked at her. He rose to his feet, sniffed the air, then shimmered into the man. He looked frightened. "You can smell it too. Fire."

Marlene was instantly on her feet in killing mode, sniffing at the air. "Dammit, you're right. It's ahead of us. What do we do now?"

"You're asking me?"

"I've never faced a forest fire, have you?"

"Several. We need to find a river, lake, or a deep cave. Failing that we need to get around it."

"That ridge, could we see it from there?"

"Possibly, but it'll take us closer to it."

"I can travel faster than you can, even as the bear. Stay here, I'll go." Before he could object, she was gone.

Grumbling to himself, he changed back to the bear and set out after her. He found her at the top of the ridge swearing like a trooper. High above the hawk called then soared away. They were nearly surrounded by fire. He shimmered back into the man as he took in the scene before him.

The fire was a ways off as yet, but their only avenue of escape seemed to be towards the town in the near distance. There was a small river between them and the town, but it was much too small to stop the oncoming inferno. "Come on," he barked then shimmered back into the bear.

He headed down the slope as fast as he could. Terrified, Marlene stayed right behind him. She'd been burned as a witch once, fire was about the only thing that could frighten her. Marlene had no idea what he was doing, but she trusted that action of any kind was better than waiting to be burned alive.

The sounds of the roaring fire began to reach her ears and she realized he was leading her right at the fire. She slapped his rump hard and stopped running. The huge bear spun with alarming speed and snarled, but she stepped right up to its face. "What the fuck are you doing? We're running right at the fire."

"I know," he replied, as he shimmered back into the man. "Look, there's no way to escape it. There's a town this way, that means men fighting the fire. It also means they'll be seeing lots of forest animals fleeing past them. If we run past them we can get behind whatever fire breaks they've built. It's that or get burned alive."

"That might work for you as the bear, but what about me?"

"When we get close go back into little girl mode. You're a hiker trapped by the fire. They'll let you through, you can follow my scent and we can hook up again. If you have a better idea talk fast."

She gazed into his eyes for a moment, then relented. "I don't. Let's go."

He shifted back into the bear and set out again. Soon they were feeling the heat and hearing the roar of the flames. Wild animals were racing towards them, and the bear changed course, angling away from the fire, but still moving towards the town.

Marlene caught the high-pitched roar of a chain saw and shifted back to the woman. In this form she couldn't keep up with the bear, but she tried. Smoke was billowing over her as, choking, she reached the fire line. "Jesus Christ, there's a woman. Over here! Over here!" She stumbled toward the sound of the voice.

Marlene was swept up in strong arms and carried to a truck loading up with men. They were being pushed back by the fire. She was put in the back of the truck with a group of soot-stained men and a small canister of oxygen was pressed to her face. She inhaled greedily of the sweet life-giving gas.

"Miss, what the hell were you doing out there? Was there anybody else with you?"

"We were out camping," she gasped. "My boyfriend ran from the fire, but I couldn't keep up and he left me behind."

"The dirty bastard," growled one of the men. "Are you all right, girl? We have to set up a new fire line, but we can get you a ride back to town. Will you be okay on your own?"

Marlene gave him a smile and wiped the soot from her face. "I'll be fine, just get me away from that fire."

"There'll be somebody running supplies out from town," he replied. "You can catch a ride back with them. Check in with the sheriff's office or the hospital. They'll know if your boyfriend has been found or not."

The truck pulled into a makeshift headquarters. Marlene thanked the men who'd saved her and caught a ride back to town with a woman driving a sandwich truck. She got dropped off at a gas station where she cleaned herself up as best she could.

She asked if there was a place she could rent a car. There wasn't and she was directed to an old car lot. In the end she used her credit card to pay far too much for an old wreck, but she needed wheels.

Marlene drove to the side of town away from the fire, parked and called to report in. "Tommy here."

"You sound busy, Tommy."

"Hi, Miss Marlene. Yes, we're setting up in the new castle. The king is out with Mr. Walker inspecting the new farm."

"Tommy, what the hell are you talking about?"

"Sorry, you've been out of touch for too long I guess. The king's moved the entire court to a castle further north, well away from New York and prying eyes. We're setting up now and Eric just arrived with the were-wolves. We ..."

"Tommy, just tell me where I have to go."

"I'll send the coordinates to your phone. Give us a couple of days then check in, maybe someone can pick you up. Will you be all right until then?"

"Sure, we'll just kick back and roast marshmallows in the forest fire." His sputtered response was lost as she closed the connection and returned the phone to her pocket.

Marlene looked back over her shoulder and saw the glow of the fire against the sky. "That damned fire will burn this town to the ground. Come on, Torvil, where the hell are you?" She was still pacing as the bear came out of the trees and shimmered into the man.

"Let's get the hell out of here before that fire catches us," he grumbled, as he shook the ash from his hair.

Sunrise found them still in the traffic jam of people fleeing the fire. He was grumbling and she was getting irritable. Marlene needed to feed. "Just stay down on the back seat and keep that blanket over you. As soon as we get out of this mess we'll hit the highway then find a motel where you can order a pizza and I can eat the delivery guy. Now shut the hell up." Wisely, he obeyed.

Marlene hadn't gone far when she heard a strange sound coming from the back seat. "Is that snoring? It is, it's snoring. Good god, I'm up here trying to keep us alive and he's asleep in the back. I should bite him for that." Still muttering, she drove on. However, she didn't get nearly as far as she'd like.

The car coasted to a stop at the flashing lights. Marlene stepped out and gave the policeman her best smile. "What's going on, officer?"

"Ma'am, there's a forest fire."

"I know, I'm trying to get away from it."

"Yeah, well, the wind came up and the damned thing changed course, jumped the fire break, and took off. You're heading right at it again. Now, I need you to turn around. There's a road about a mile back that way, take a left there and go on about fifteen miles. That'll put you at the highway east. I'd suggest going east a good long ways."

"I'll go right to the ocean," she sighed.

"Dang fine idea," he chuckled. "Keep an eye on the news, it'll let you know when it's safe to return."

"Thank you, officer," she said as she got back in the car. "You're a life saver."

"All my pleasure, ma'am. You go on, now, get far as away from here as you can." He waved as she drove back the way she'd come.

"You've stopped snoring, so I know you're awake. Did you hear any of that?"

Torvil chuckled and sat up. "All of it. Seems like my luck is running true to form."

"Yours and mine both," she grumbled, as she made the turn onto the new road. It was a lonely stretch through the forest and Marlene was getting nervous.

"You all right, Marlene?"

She sighed and gripped the wheel tighter. "I'm fine."

"Now why don't I believe that."

"Because I'm lying through my teeth. I'm scared, Torvil. I know I can revive if we're caught by the fire, but I was burned as a witch once. That was no damn fun at all, and ..."

Her voice caught and she stopped speaking. Suddenly a gentle hand gave her shoulder a squeeze. "It's all right, little sister, I understand what you mean. I've been caught in a forest fire twice in my life. You can come back from it, but the pain is indescribable, and coming back leaves you hungry beyond belief, but in a place with no food.

"Look, we're in good shape here. You've got us well ahead of the fire, it probably won't get this far anyway, and even if it does we'll be long gone before that happens."

With a shuddering sigh, Marlene got control of her fears. She patted the hand on her shoulder and nodded. A few minutes later she saw the highway and the traffic jam that had it at a standstill. "Fuck! What the hell else can go wrong?"

"Easy girl. Just pull over and we'll take to the woods again."

"Torvil, we can't ..."

"We can cover a lot more ground in the woods than those fools will on that highway. Stay with me now, little sister. Pull over."

She did. Marlene turned in her seat to look into his eyes. "Look, I'm scared to death here. I can go a few more days but then I'll have to feed. You have previous experience, and I'm losing my ability to function rationally. Take the lead and get us the hell out of this mess."

"Your people are well north of here, and the fire is to the west. We'll head northeast and you can keep track of the fire with that magic phone until we can get picked up. If I remember the geography right, we should reach a river in a day or two. Once we cross that we'll be in the clear."

They slipped out of the car and into the trees. Torvil went bear and Marlene shifted onto vampire once more to keep up. It was a moonlit night, so they were able to travel. Dawn was breaking as they stopped to rest.

Marlene was instantly asleep and Torvil sighed as he watched her slowly return to the woman. "At least the damned fire stopped whatever was tracking us. With any luck it's dead. The hawk seems to have stayed with us, though. Startin' to wonder what that's about. Is the king's agent keeping an eye on us maybe?

"Poor girl's exhausted and scared to death," he mused. "Ah hell, I couldn't light out now even if I wanted to, I can't leave her like this. Besides, I'm starting to think her people might be my only hope. If I slip away I'll end up in bear mode for the rest of forever."

He got a wistful smile on his face as he watched her sleep. "Girl, you're more like my Dorrie than I'd care to admit. I'll get you back to your people. Hell, I guess fifty thousand years or more is a good lifespan. If they decide to kill me, I've still had a good run."

She whimpered in her sleep and he lightly patted her shoulder. She sighed and rolled over.

It was late in the afternoon when Marlene awakened, the bear lying nearby. His eyes opened the instant she stirred. "I smell smoke," she said, wide eyed and frightened.

"It's all right girl," said Torvil, as he shimmered back into the man. "That smell will carry for half a continent from a fire of that size. We're still good. Come on." He shimmered back into the bear and started out.

The bear pushed hard through the rest of the day, and she remained in full vampire mode to keep up. At this pace she wouldn't last too many more days before she collapsed. Suddenly they startled a deer and it leaped away, but the vampire slammed into it, flipping it through the air before knocking it to the ground. She drank greedily until there was no more to be had. She backed away so the bear could feed on the meat.

When the bear had eaten his fill they set out again. Clouds covered the moon, so they stopped at dark and settled down under a tree. Torvil shimmered back into the man. "So, how are you doing? Did you get enough blood?"

"No, not really. I can survive on animal blood for years if I have to, and I have in the past, but it's human blood I need to completely return to full strength. We'll stick to the trees; I can make it this way until we get clear."

He nodded thoughtfully.

"How about you?" she asked. "Did you get enough?"

"Not quite, but it'll do for a while. We'll stay hard on the move until we cross a wide river, or get a couple of days of heavy rain. Once the fire danger's passed we can slow down and rebuild our reserves."

"Works for me. Torvil, I'm sorry to come unglued on you like that. Fire scares the crap out of me, and I'm willing to admit it."

He chuckled and patted her hand. "It's all right, little sister, there had to be a weakness in there somewhere. We've all got one."

Marlene gave him a shy smile of gratitude. "Oh yeah, what's your weakness?"

"Pretty girls, can't resist them, I'm just putty in their hands, but scary vampires frighten the lights out of me."

Her sweet laughter floated lightly through the trees bringing a wide smile to his face. "You're a bad man, Torvil the Bear."

"I've been told that many times. You settle down for a rest now, the bear can keep watch."

The next morning they climbed a ridge and Marlene tried her phone. She started to swear like a sailor and Torvil chuckled. "Marlene, that's not ladylike language."

"Oh shut the fuck up," she replied, and then started to laugh.

"Battery dead?" he grinned.

"As a doornail. Well, at least I can't see any fire close by. I can't sense that hunter either."

"No, I think you got us a big enough lead with that old car. Wouldn't like to bet on it though. We should keep moving. What do you want to do about the phone?"

"There's nothing I can do about it, big brother. Let's keep moving northeast until we hit a city, then I'll go hunting, first for food and then for a way to charge up the phone so we can connect with the king. Damnit it all, Harald owes me big time for this one."

Torvil grinned and shimmered back into the bear. They set out again into the seemingly endless forest.

Far behind them a lone hunter searched for their trail. He'd lost a lot of time when he got pressed into service fighting the fire. High overhead he too was being watched.

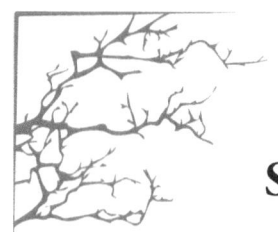

Setting Up Shop

Tommy was fussing with the electronic connections as the king entered the great hall. It pleased him immensely that this one actually looked like a great hall. Tommy gave a mutter of victory as the big screen came to life. He flicked the screen a few times then settled on the news report of the forest fire further south. It had completely obliterated an entire town and was consuming everything in its path. He started to swear under his breath.

"Tommy, what is it?"

"Huh? Oh, hi Sire, didn't hear you come in. Sire, it's the forest fire. Marlene's last known location was right here."

The red dot from Tommy's laser pointer rested in the heart of the fire. Harald swallowed hard. "If she's perished in that fire she'll need blood and lots of it when she returns from the lands beyond. Can we get to those coordinates?"

"No, Sire, the fire's destroyed everything in its path, and the National Guard is there trying to organize a full evacuation of the surrounding area. There's no way for us to get near it."

Harald's shoulders slumped and he sighed as he sank into his huge chair. "Sire, perhaps Queen Sally could help."

"Yes, of course. Good thinking, Tommy. I think she's ..."

"Right behind you," said the queen, as she leaned over to kiss his cheek. "I sensed your mood and came to see if I could help. Tell me what's happened."

"It's the forest fire down south, Sally my love. We're afraid Marlene is caught in the middle of it and there's no way for us to get help to her.

89

If she's been taken by the fire she could revive then starve two or three times before she could manage to feed herself and contact us."

"Oh dear, that's not good at all. Let me see if I can get anything." She sat gracefully in the plush chair beside his and began a series of deep breaths. She chanted softly for a few moments then began to call Marlene's name.

Both the king and Tommy waited while she meditated. A wave of relief washed over them both as Sally chuckled and opened her eyes. "Marlene and the were-bear escaped the fire, but only just. It was close, and Marlene is still a bit frightened. She's also very tired and hungry.

"They're on the move and the were-bear is traveling with a seriously cranky vampire. Apparently the battery on her phone ran down and that was the last straw.

"They're fine, Harald, and heading this way through the forest. They're a long way off as yet, but they're safe and moving this way.

"I sense a bond growing between them, for in spite of the danger implied, he teased her and she didn't bite him, although she did threaten to. I believe we can relax; they've left the fire behind."

"That's good news indeed," said the king. "If I'd known how hard this would be I'd have gone myself."

"Harald?"

"I first met Marlene in France. She'd been burned as a witch. I happened upon the scene as she was dying, screaming, and shifting to vampire and back to human. The people were all chanting 'Die, demon, die.'

"When the fire had burned down and the people went home, I followed the priest and his helper as they buried her corpse and performed a ceremony over the grave. When she awakened and dug her way out of that grave I was waiting with both the priest and his accomplice for her to eat. She drained them dry and recovered. I stayed with her for a while until she was ready to go on her own again."

"You've got a soft spot for her, don't you?"

"Yes, I confess I do think of her as a little sister. She's not like the rest of us. Marlene wasn't made vampire because she begged for it, wanted it, as the rest of us did. She was changed quite by accident. Fortunately for her, Mother was there and helped her gain control of the killing lust.

"Sadly, she went her own way before she mastered a few of the subtleties of society. Mother taught her control, but it was I who taught her how to hunt and remain unseen in the cities."

"Well, you can put your mind at rest, she's on her way home and bringing you a were-bear. However, I suspect you're going to have some sucking up to do. She'll want at least three weeks in a bath for a start."

Harald chuckled at that. "I'll just bet. The girl can be a bit of a princess, all right. Ah well, forewarned is fore armed, as they say. Do we have her apartment set up yet?"

"They're finished with the others and are working on hers now, I think," said Sally. "I'll go check, if you like?"

"Thank you, my sweet. Please make sure it's ready and waiting for a full pampering of the girl when she arrives. See if Gudrun has any spare bottles of that blood to put in the room as well."

"On it," said the queen, as she rose and patted his broad shoulder. "Oh, Harald, I got the sense something was hunting her as well. It's probably just the hunters they've been avoiding all along. Nothing to worry about." He sighed with relief again as she left the great hall.

"Tommy, what's our status on the rest of the relocation?"

A few swift clicks and Tommy had a spreadsheet on the screen. "Two more days then we close the purchase on the two farms. Once we have the sales finalized we can begin to get Mr. Walker settled in."

"How is Bill, I haven't seen him for a couple of days?"

Tommy chuckled at that. "Sire, he and Olla walk the perimeter of the farms every morning. He takes his job of our lookout seriously. Personally, I think he's watching for Marlene."

"Could be, Tommy. Why is Olla accompanying him?"

Tommy grinned. "Bill made some comment about getting a dog to walk with him so he'd have company. Olla volunteered. The poor guy nearly crapped himself when she stripped off and shifted into wolf form. Now the wolf meets him at the door every morning and they walk the farm."

The king chuckled and shook his head. "Tommy, some days that wife of yours is all mischief."

"It's worse than you think, Sire. I believe she's doing this so I have to get the children's breakfast and clean up afterward. Yes, she's all mischief."

"I think you like it."

"Don't tell Olla."

"My lips are sealed. What else have we got on the go?"

"Miss Gudrun's people in Europe have decided on your castle in Germany and are refurbishing it as a bolt hole for us. They've also found another as a backup if needed. Terry and his team are back in New York tying off any loose ends and shutting down any overly curious authority types. Miss Gina and Marco are actively shutting down any underworld curiosity."

"Did Mother go with Terry?"

"She did, Sire, but Clyde, Amanda, and Clara remained here to help ease the transition. I have to say, Clara loves the new lab toys you let her buy."

Harald nodded and smiled. "What about you, Tommy? Are you able to function properly here?"

"I was having some reception issues, but Georg and Igor set up an antenna for me on that high ridge behind the castle. That cleared up everything nicely and I'm good to go."

"Excellent."

"Sire, may I ask ...?"

"The interviews? Yes, we accepted three of the applicants. They should arrive for their introduction to service later today. As king that will be my task. How are the wolves doing?"

"They've settled into the number three bomb shelter. Georg says they love it, it makes them a fine den and they can access the forest through the tunnels."

"Then I'm well pleased with that. How is the library coming?"

"Ah, we've got a delay there, Sire. The truck with the load of books had mechanical issues and is awaiting repairs. We should have everything here by the end of the week."

"Gudrun's people?"

"All settled in and they've secured the premises. Miss Gudrun has promised a full report in person as soon as all the electronic security is fully activated. I'll give you a full briefing on the rest once I've gone over it all."

"Excellent, Tommy, excellent. It looks as though things are going smoothly, so I have time for a bit of sword practice before the new employees arrive."

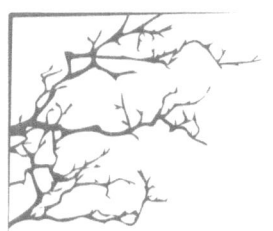

Hiking Trail

Two boys with fishing poles hid in the trees and watched as the giant bear climbed out of the river and shook his coat, sending a spray of water for several feet in all directions.

A moment later a demon with a woman's body followed him from the river. She shook out her hair and snarled as the bear shimmered into a man. "Can you see what I see?"

"Yes, and I smell the blood," she replied. "Into the trees now." The man disappeared into the trees and she followed close behind. As soon as the two demons were out of sight the boys ran for home. They were unaware of the vampire following them.

Marlene fought the burning need for blood and stayed back out of sight. She'd have to drain both children to get a meal, but they should have parents nearby. It was late in the day and all she had to do was be patient. Following the sounds of their flight, as well as the scent of blood, she struggled for control.

They burst from the trees and into a farmyard, shouting for their parents. Marlene slunk around the side and hid herself in the barn. The animals began to mill about nervously as they scented the predator.

Excited voices carried easily to her ears from outside. "I'm telling you, Pa, we saw it. The bear changed into a caveman and the demon talked to it. They came out of the river."

"Stop it now," roared an angry male voice. "There's no such things as demons or giant bears. I don't know what you saw, but ..." There was a sudden terrified squealing and a boar fled from the forest with a huge bear right behind it. They crossed the farmyard and vanished into the woods on the other side.

The man ran toward the house. "Merilee, fetch my rifle, hurry." In a few more moments the man was in the trees hunting the bear. He could hear the squeals of the boar as the bear killed it.

He burst into the clearing and raised his rifle, but something slammed into him from behind. He was face down on the ground with an animal on his back. Needle sharp fangs bit deeply into his neck, and he struggled weakly as the vampire slaked her thirst.

Finally she thrust herself off him and rose to her feet. "You should have listened to your son," she growled. He crawled away from her as she spoke to the bear that was feasting on the dead pig. "Nice diversion."

Before he could reach his rifle she caught him and dragged him away. He whimpered and tried to shrink away from her, but a voice from a distant hell stopped him cold. *"Be still. Tell me where we are."*

"In the woods."

Her snarl showed her fangs and he whimpered again as she took a step towards him. *"What state?"*

"New York."

"When we leave you will fire three shots into the air. When asked, you will say that you came upon a bear killing a pig. You frightened it off. You saw nothing else, just an average sized bear killing a pig. You will remember nothing else."

The bear tore off a haunch of meat and disappeared into the trees. Marlene followed and soon they heard the three shots. She nodded and trotted off. "We should keep moving in case he sends for hunters. At least we've reached New York."

They continued on until dark then stopped. The sky was covered by heavy clouds so they decided not to travel. As they settled down she noticed the bear sniffing the air. "What is it?" She tested the air herself, but scented only forest. "What?"

The bear shimmered into the man. "I think I smell something special."

"You do?"

"The land, the smells, something vaguely familiar. Yup, there's a campsite nearby."

Marlene sat up straighter and tested the air again. Yes, there it was, just a faint whiff then gone, but it had been there. Hot dogs. "Stay put." She was gone into the night, her feral night vision serving her well.

It took her a while, but she found it, a campsite. There were people sitting around a fire roasting hot dogs. Trying to ignore the sound of blood rushing through their veins, she focused on the voices.

"I'm tired of this already," whined one woman.

"Oh for fuck sake," sighed another. "We haven't even reached the Appalachian Trail yet. It's only another seventy miles from here to the border on the trail. We can do it easily in a week. That was the idea, right?"

"Yeah, why are you so bummed out all of a sudden?"

"My phone's dead," sighed the first woman.

"Oh no, oh my god, disaster ..."

"Shut up."

"Look, I've got a solar charger in my pack. First thing tomorrow I'll hang it out on the backpack and charge your phone for you, okay?"

"You can do that?"

"Sure can. If we get a sunny day it'll be fully charged in a few hours."

"Sweet. Okay, if you can do that I'll be all right."

"Jesus, you are so attached to that frigging phone. Wouldn't hurt you to be offline for a few weeks."

They continued to talk, but Marlene withdrew further into the trees to wait. Fiercely controlling the blood lust, she waited with the inborn patience of the hunting cat. After all, she was part saber-toothed tiger, and they were ambush hunters. Patience was their hallmark.

Time passed and the hikers retired to their tents. Deep in the starless night a predator slipped into one of the tents. The man awakened as the fangs of the cat bit deep, but his struggles soon ceased.

When he finally lay still a terrible voice whispered in his ear. *"You had a nightmare; it has left you exhausted. Sleep now, and forget I was ever here."*

He closed his eyes and she slipped out of the tent, the solar charger clutched in her hand.

Torvil awakened at daylight to see the girl sleeping beside him. He shimmered into the man and went behind a tree to relieve himself. When he returned she was awake. "Well, you're looking better than I've seen you in a while. You get your tank all topped up?"

She laughed with delight. "Yes I did. First the farmer, and then a camper last night, and I'm all brand new. I also learned some useful things."

"Oh, do tell."

"Okay, first, we're near the Appalachian hiking trail, it runs north and will drop us out near the coordinates Tommy sent us. It's still a hell of a hike from here, but a lot easier traveling. We'll have to stay out of sight of hikers, and circle around a few towns, but we can cover a lot more ground every day."

"Yeah, and you can feed off the hikers so it'll just be me we need to find food for."

"The hikers will be carrying food for themselves. We can forage off that. You'll have to eat human food, but you'll survive."

He grimaced and rolled his eyes at that. "If you say so. What's that gadget you've got there?"

"That, dear brother bear, is a solar charger. See, I've already got my phone plugged in. If we leave it in the sun I'll be all charged up in a few hours."

"Oh, now that's pure bit of treasure. All right, let's find that hiking trail and get started. Once we hit easy traveling I'll forage a bit. The blueberries should be coming ripe in the mountains about now."

"The idea of ration bars isn't appealing?"

"Oh hell no." She laughed at that, bringing a smile to his face. "Girl, it's good to see you well fed again."

"Thanks, but now we have to get you topped up too. Here, you relax with the solar charger while I see if I can find you some meat." He shimmered back into the bear and she disappeared into the forest. She was back in less than an hour with the carcass of a deer over her shoulder.

Once he had eaten his fill they set out. By the end of day they'd tracked the campers onto the Appalachian Trail. They passed them by in the night. By dawn they were well onto the mountain trail, but the going had been much easier. They slipped off the path and found a place to rest for the day.

Early the next morning they were up and away. With Torvil traveling in bear mode and Marlene in full vampire, they covered distance at three times the speed of the hikers behind them, and ever the watcher from above paced them.

As the sun rose high and the day heated up, they sought shade for a rest. She pulled out her freshly charged phone and called. She was pleasantly surprised that she actually got reception.

"Tommy here."

"Tommy, it's Marlene."

"Miss Marlene, it's good to hear from you. We were afraid you'd been caught in that big forest fire down south."

"Close, but we managed to escape. Listen, Tommy, we're just inside the New York state border. We're on the Appalachian hiking trail. We can make better time now."

"Do you need a pick up?"

"No, we'll keep going. The traveling is easier now and I get the impression you folks are quite busy these days."

"We're almost fully settled in, but we do need a while yet to get it all straightened out. Are you sure you'll be okay?"

"We're good. If that changes I'll look for a place Eric can set the plane down."

"Ah, they're in Europe right now."

"Harald wants a back up bolt hole?"

Tommy chuckled at that. "Yes, ma'am. They've got a place set up, but he sent Miss Gudrun and company there to double check everything then to look for a back up to that. They should be home late next week."

He cringed slightly as he heard the deep sigh. "All right, Tommy, I'll check in again in another week. Keep the home fires burning, we'll be home by Christmas." With that she broke the connection and he dropped into a chair and sighed.

"Tommy, are you all right?"

"Oh, sorry Sire," said Tommy, as he leaped to his feet, but the king waved him back to his chair. Harald sank into his favorite chair and quirked an eyebrow at Tommy. "That was Miss Marlene on the phone, Sire. They've just crossed into New York State on the Appalachian Hiking Trail. I said the plane was in Europe right now and she said not to worry, they'd be home by Christmas."

King Harald grinned at that. "Tommy, my friend, right now I'm happy that she's out on the trail and not in the room with us."

"Amen to that, Sire. Amen to that. I feel sorry for the poor bear."

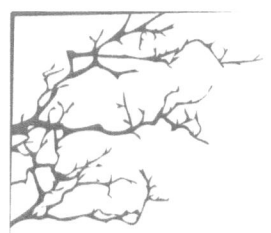

Hiking

Quarreling bitterly, the young couple hurried on through the heavy rain. There was a shelter near where they could camp and make a fire, dry themselves out. The small woman was berating her stocky companion for holding them back.

She was the avid hiker; her boyfriend wasn't. The new boots hurt his feet, his muscles were stiff, he was soaked, and regretted lying to her to get a date. He was miserable and letting it show. She, on the other hand, was ready to throttle him to shut him up.

Darkness was falling when the shelter loomed out of the rain. There were two other people already there and there was a cheery fire going. "Oh thank god," sighed the young man, as he threw himself down by the fire.

"Jesus, Harvey," said the girl, as she sat and shucked off her jacket. "Sorry about that, folks, I think it's his first overnight hike. I'm Jean and this is Harvey. Can we build up your fire a bit more to dry out?" Her focus was on the welcoming fire and so was her companion's.

"Help yourself," replied the man in the shadows.

The woman threw another stick of firewood onto the blaze and stirred the coals to make them hotter. She and her companion sat huddled over the fire, warming themselves. "You folks are lifesavers," said Harvey, his teeth chattering.

"All our pleasure," replied a soft musical voice, but there was something in that voice that caught the woman's attention and sent a shiver up her spine. She raised her eyes and took a closer look at the other two people in the shelter with them.

The man was short with heavy features, but unlike her date, he was heavily muscled with a thick layer of dark body hair. It slowly sank into her tired brain that the man appeared to be naked. She swallowed hard and shifted her gaze to the woman.

The girl was about her size with red hair and freckles, but she was clothed in rags. Something about her made the woman nervous. Slowly she raised her eyes to the girl's face and saw it begin to change. Meeting the woman's gaze she saw feral cat's eyes fixed on her like a predator's eyes fixed on prey.

Transfixed by those eyes, she swallowed and spoke, trying to force her muscles to respond to the danger. "What are you?"

She began to tremble in fear as the woman rose to her feet and spoke a single word. "Vampire." Jean had no time to react before she was seized in powerful claw tipped hands and sharp fangs pierced her throat.

Hearing a suckling sound, the man brought his eyes up from the fire. What he thought he saw was a woman nuzzling the neck of his girlfriend. "Aw for fuck sake, what the hell do you two think you're...?" He got no further as the vampire thrust the limp woman aside and leaped on him.

He howled in terror as she sank her fangs into his neck. The woman tried to crawl away while the demon from a nightmare fed on her companion. She had barely reached the trail when the naked man scooped her up in his arms and carried her back into the shelter. "Stay here by the fire," he said, as he set her down. "You'll catch your death out there."

He set her down beside her companion who was now staring at the vampire licking the last drops of blood from her lips. He trembled as she rose to her feet. *"Remove your clothing and get into your sleeping bags."* Fearfully they obeyed. *"Sleep now, and rest. You will hear nothing until morning."*

They closed their eyes and Torvil grinned. "Feeling better?"

"Much. I get seriously cranky when I'm hungry."

"Really? I hadn't noticed." She laughed and slapped at his arm. "So, what are you going to do with them now?"

"Do you see anything special about them, brother bear?"

"Not really," he replied, as he threw another stick on the fire. "What did I miss?"

"They're about the same size as we are. We're getting near a populated area now and should travel as humans until we pass the town. We'll dress in their clothes and carry on. Check the back packs and see if there's anything you can eat in there."

"Well I'll be danged," chuckled Torvil, as he rummaged through the man's pack. "This boy carries good stuff. All she's got is protein bars, but here's a sub sandwich."

Marlene smiled as he ate the sandwich and drank the bottle of water with it. "So, here's the plan, in the morning I give these two a story to tell about thieves, and then we set out in their clothes. Once we reach the high ground again, I'll carry your clothes in the backpack so you can travel as the bear."

"That works for me. Girl, that voice of command of yours is a trick worth the learning."

"Came with the change," she smiled. "It's a great tool, but too easy to get dependent on it."

"We could steal their car and make a getaway."

"We're well clear of the trouble spot down south, and I want to stay out of sight. The king's moved all the people to a new stronghold, I don't want to do anything that might draw attention to that. I'd rather take a while longer to get there and do it quietly."

"That makes sense, girl. Get some sleep now, I'll keep watch." She nodded then settled down beside the two people in sleeping bags. She hadn't said anything, but he knew she'd sensed it too, the hunter was on their trail again. "Whoever that is," mused Torvil, "he's not entirely human. This could become a problem."

Not so far away, on their back trail, a hunter knelt on the ground. He poked and peered at the soil, sniffed at it and the air as well, and the whole time muttering softly to himself. "Sometimes bear, sometimes man, and a woman who's not a woman. Be very wary here, Cher, these demons be dangerous. Best to take them by surprise."

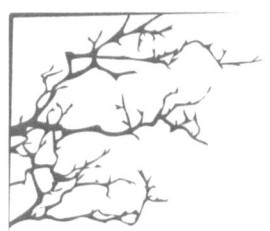

Poisoned

The Queen of the Vampire Clan awoke screaming, her husband trying to calm and comfort her. "Sally, Sally, easy my love, easy. You were dreaming, sweetheart. It was only a dream. Hush now, sweet Sally, hush and let me hold you."

"Harald, oh gods, Harald, that was so real. We have to warn Marlene."

"Warn Marlene?"

"It was in the dream, something evil, dangerous. Harald, I need to calm down then take another look at this thing."

"Are you certain that's wise right now?"

"Yes, I have to know, I have to. If this thing following Marlene is what I saw in the dream then she's in grave danger."

"All right, my sweet, but I want you to have some tea and settle down a bit before you go looking for this thing, whatever it is."

They arose and headed for the kitchen. A young woman was already there with the kettle on the stove. "I thought you might want some tea," she smiled. "Shall I make some toast to go with that?"

"Yes please," replied Sally. "How did you know we were awake?"

"I've only been here a couple of days, but it's easy to see you're both night owls. The rest of the humans have already been up and had breakfast."

"And you were up to cook that breakfast?" asked the king.

"Yes, Sire. Sorry, but I'm an incurable morning person."

"I knew you were the right choice for the job, Elaine, but we'll hire a full time cook soon. Thank you for standing in."

The girl smiled her delight. "Would you prefer to take your tea in the great hall or in your study?"

"The study this time," replied Sally. They went to the study, and she was soon there with a tray for them.

She set the tray on the coffee table then withdrew. Sally took a long sip of her tea then nibbled at the toast. Harald sat beside her, quietly waiting. "The man following Marlene is a non-human, or at least he was in the dream."

"Another non-human?"

"Yes, but we don't want that one here, and I doubt we could keep it confined for any length of time. Give me a moment, I want another look at this thing." She folded her hands in her lap and began a series of deep breathing exercises. As she allowed the trance to take her a snarl of rage crossed her exquisite features. A few moments later she shook off the trance.

Her eyes wild, Sally reached for her tea with a trembling hand. "Sally, what did you see?"

With a visible effort she regained control of her emotions. "This thing, I won't call it a man, is evil. It hunts and kills for food, eating it raw, often well before the victim is dead. It has eaten humans before. It's fast, deadly, an efficient hunter/killer, and it's tenacious when on the hunt. It tracks by scent as much as by sight.

"I believe it may be part snake, for its bite is poisonous. Harald, it'll kill her, for it believes it'll gain her strength by eating her beating heart. We have to warn her."

"Indeed we do. Will you be all right here for a while? I'll send that new magic cook in with more tea and toast." She nodded weakly and shuddered before taking another sip of the tea.

The king strode into the great hall, his eyes searching for Tommy. As usual he found him at the controls of some piece of technology or other. "Tommy, see if you can raise Marlene for me."

"Sire?"

"Quickly now, her life may depend upon it."

"Yes, Sire, I work as we speak." Sadly, his efforts bore no fruit. "Sorry, Sire, she must be out of range of a tower."

"Dammit all to hell and back. Keep trying, Tommy. As soon as you have her on the line put her through to me."

"Yes, Sir. I'll set the modem to auto dial every thirty seconds until we get an answer."

WHILE THE KING PACED and worried, Marlene was once again cursing the fact she couldn't get any reception. The bear had wandered off looking for blueberries and she was distracted by the phone.

Suddenly every instinct she had screamed of danger as the hawk cried out overhead. She shifted to vampire mode and spun around just as the body slammed into her, knocking her to the ground. His fangs had missed her throat, but he did get a gash into her arm and a slash across her abdomen with the hunting knife. He'd have preferred to shoot her first, but he'd lost his rifle in the forest fire. He was down to hunting the hard way.

It wasn't clean for him either. She threw him aside, tearing a great gash out of his side as she did. He leaped to his feet and dodged away, but she got another piece of him with her claws. He hissed in pain and fled into the forest.

Marlene whimpered in agony and sank to the ground. She could feel the poison coursing through her veins, burning like a fire, inhibiting her ability to heal the wounds. She tore off a piece of her shirt to bind her upper arm, hoping to prevent the spread of more poison.

The sun was hot and the poison was doing its job. She tried to rise and find shelter, but she stumbled and sank to the ground again. She was delirious when Torvil found her there.

Within the trees the hunter saw her fall and rejoiced. "So, LeBlanc's bite will bring you down, Blood Drinker. You are stronger than I thought, Cher. I hurt from your claws, but now I feast and grow strong once again." He started to move forward, but stopped. The bear had found her. He was in no condition to fight the bear and he knew it. He slunk back into the forest. From high above the hawk watched him carefully.

Torvil smelled something wrong in the blood scent. He hurried back to Marlene and found her huddled by the trail as though freezing, but it was quite hot outside. She should have found shelter by now. She was almost unconscious, and not making sense. Shifting to the man he scooped her up and carried her off the trail and into the shade of the trees.

"What happened, girl?"

It took her a minute to focus. "Huh? Oh gods I hurt. It bit me, Torvil. The fucker has fangs, poison ...can't heal ...need ... blood ..." Her mind wandered off again and he sighed then shifted into the bear. There was no further sign of the hunter in the air, and he sensed that she had hurt the creature too. Torvil shifted back into the man.

"Dammit, she needs blood, but there's not a hiker anywhere near, and I dare not leave her alone. Can't let her bite me either, not in the state she's in, she'd never get herself stopped in time. That leaves only one option as far as I can see."

He opened the backpack she'd been carrying and took out the water bottle then drank all of its contents. With a sigh he took up the small knife and made a cut on his arm, carefully collecting the blood into the bottle. When it was full he set it down then bandaged the cut.

Scooping up the container of his own blood he put his arm around her shoulders and held it to her lips. "Drink your medicine, now, little sister. Drink it all."

At the first taste of the blood her senses kicked in and she drank greedily until it was all gone. In mere moments her eyes cleared, and her wounds began to seal. She was breathing deeply and passed back the container. "Is there more?"

"I can fill it one more time only. Just a minute." He pulled off the bandage and reopened the wound. She watched as he filled the container and passed it to her. She drank it all while watching him re-bandage the cut on his arm.

"You gave me your blood. Why?"

"You were fading on me, and there was nobody else around. I was afraid to leave you in case it came back. So, it's bite is poison, a non-human then."

"Yes. It attacked, but I hurt it as well. I have no idea how easily it can heal, but I did manage to hurt it. It won't be so eager to come at me again."

Torvil nodded and sighed. "Will you be all right now?"

"No. I can feel the poison still in my blood stream, but both my healing factor and yours are fighting it. I can function now, but I need to feed, and I'll need time to heal. Torvil, if that thing comes at you, kill it quick, don't let it bite you."

Again he nodded. "What did it look like?"

"A small man, but as fast as I am, and terribly strong. It doesn't have claws, but it does have fangs and it used a knife. When I catch that bastard I'm gonna drink him dry."

"Don't do it, girl. You don't want to have any of that thing's blood in you. As soon as you can travel we'll find you a couple of hikers to eat."

She chuckled at that. "How about you, Torvil? You gave me a couple of pints of the best. Are you all right? Can you function? Can you travel?"

"I need to feed too, girl, but I can function, and yes, I can travel. Having said that, we need to stay close to each other. Neither one of us is battle ready at the moment."

"You're right about that. Torvil, what you did for me was above and beyond the call of duty, I owe you. Nobody has ever ..."

"I know, girl. I have to say, this older brother job is a lot tougher than I thought." Her silvery laughter brought a wide grin to his face. "We should rest here until dark then look for a full campsite. You can eat the campers and I can raid the backpacks."

"Agreed. Torvil, once we're back to full health you know what we have to do."

"We have to hunt that bastard down and kill it," he growled. "I know. We'll make an end of him. We can't lead that thing anywhere near your king's new castle."

They returned to the trail as the day faded into darkness. The well-traveled path was easy to follow, and they stay close together. Torvil stayed in bear form, constantly testing the air, listening with all his power. The hunter was following them but keeping his distance.

All through the night they walked, but Marlene was struggling. She stopped to rest more frequently as the night wore on. Worse yet, they didn't find a shelter with people in it. The only one they found was empty.

Marlene eased herself to the ground inside the shelter. "I'm beat, the damned poison is dragging me down. There's no way in hell I can keep going and retain enough strength to defend myself. You go find food for yourself; I'll stay here. That thing can't get at me from behind, so I'll be fine. With any luck a hiker or two will come along and feed me."

The bear nuzzled her, gazing deeply into her eyes. Finally it licked her then turned to go. Alone, Marlene tried her phone, but there was no reception. With a snarl of frustration, she put it back in her pocket and sighed. She began deep breathing as she focused on healing her wounds. She had to slow the progress of the poison.

The sun was well up and Marlene was dozing when she became aware of the voice. She was instantly alert, her claws fully extended. It was outside the shelter, looking for an advantage, a way she couldn't defend.

"You weak now, Blood Drinker, hurting, tired. Sleep now. LeBlanc grant you rest, peace. Sleep now, sweet Blood Drinker."

"Fuck you, snake," came her reply. "You want me, come and get me."

"In time, Blood Drinker. The poison work slow for you, but it works. LeBlanc can feel your heart slowing. LeBlanc is patient, Cher. He will come for you in time. Soon you will make LeBlanc strong." With that she heard him circling the enclosure.

Suddenly he shrieked and fled. The hawk had dived at his face and a roaring bear was right on his heels. A few moments later Torvil arrived. Seeing her raised eyebrow he shook his head. "Damn snake is sure fast. He got away, but I bloodied him up a bit. You get anybody to eat?"

"No, and that thing's right, the poison is wearing me down. Dammit, I wish there were a couple of cops or soldiers around."

"Oh? Why?" he asked, perplexed.

She sighed and sank back. "Because then I could order them to hold still while you tied them up. You could shoot me with their gun then I could eat them when I revived. I'd be completely healed and two of them would feed me enough to bring me back to full strength."

Torvil chuckled and sat beside her. "If we were near a town I could go run down Main Street naked and let them chase me back here. Sadly, we're too far away from civilization for that little adventure."

She laughed weakly and slapped at his arm. "Are you okay to watch? I really need to sleep."

"You go ahead, little sister. I'll keep watch."

"Torvil?"

"Yes?"

"If you hear any hikers coming ..."

"Yes?"

"Put your pants on." His bellow of laughter brought a smile to her face.

Darkness was falling when he heard them coming, four distinct voices. He gently shook Marlene, but she didn't wake up. Her skin was hot with fever. With a sigh Torvil rose and hid behind the wall of the shelter, locking his hands into stone hard fists.

The first man to step past him went down, unconscious from a blow to the jaw. The second fell from a punch to the gut that dropped him. The third tried to block him, but he went down as well. The fourth man fled. In a heartbeat the bear was after him.

The terrified man looked over his shoulder to see a massive bear gaining on him. He tripped and fell headlong. He screamed and fainted as the bear reached him. Torvil shimmered back into the man and threw his unconscious victim over his shoulder and returned to the shelter.

Back at the shelter one man had gotten air back into his lungs and regained his feet. Before he could decide what to do he heard a soft groan from further back in the shelter. There was a woman lying there, weakly waving an arm at him. He went to her.

"Don't try to speak. I'll get you some water then we'll get you away from here."

Her lips moved, but no sound came out. She lifted her head, and he bent forward to hear her whisper. "Thank you."

A powerful hand clamped down on the back of his neck as she shimmered into killing mode. Sharp fangs bit deep into his neck, and she moaned with delight as the hot blood squirted into her waiting mouth. She drank greedily, then slowly released him.

Whimpering in terror, he started to scramble away as the vampire crawled to one of his unconscious companions and began to feed once again. She was on the third one when a naked caveman tossed the last of his companions to her then changed into a massive bear. Horrified, the man watched as the bear turned to stand guard while the vampire fed.

The bear shimmered into the man as he heard a strong voice of command behind him. *"All of you be silent and stay still. Sleep now."*

Torvil grinned as he began to rummage through the backpacks. It was all highly concentrated foods, but it was nourishing, and he ate it all while she stood guard. "Did you get enough?" she asked over her shoulder.

"I think so. This stuff tastes like crap, but I guess it'll keep me alive." He grinned with delight at her silvery laughter. "How about you, little sister, did you get enough?"

"For now. I'm back to full strength, but I can still feel the poison within me. It's weaker, and with further feedings, my body will defeat it. However, for now I need to be careful and conserve my strength as best I can."

"So, what are we going to do with this lot?"

"They present a small problem. If we leave them here weakened the snake might come feed off them. That's a dead body or two that I don't want lying around. You didn't find any weapons in those back packs, did you?"

"One gun and everybody is carrying bear spray, why."

"Oh, it's way better to be lucky than good. You go bear, I'll deal with these guys, and then we'll head out. I'll feed on every damned hiker we find until I get this crap out of my system."

He nodded and shifted into the bear. She turned to the sleeping men. *"Wake up. Listen carefully. You used drugs then fought over the food until you saw the bear. The bear is outside. Keep your weapons at hand. Kill anything that enters the shelter. Once the sun has arisen, leave this place and find help. Stay together, beware the bear. You saw nothing else, just the bear."*

They gathered tightly together and grabbed their weapons. Marlene could hear them talking fearfully about the bear. Grinning, she joined Torvil on the trail.

They traveled steadily through the night, not pushing hard, but not resting either. All the while escorted by the hawk in the sky. As the night gave way to the dawn he shimmered back into the man. "That looks like a likely place to spend the day," he said as he pointed to a rocky outcropping. "We'll have shade, shelter, it's easily defended, and we're close to the trail for you to forage on hikers." She nodded and moved off the trail.

"So, little sister, you got any idea how we're going to deal with this snake?"

"We're going to kill it."

"Ah-huh."

"First I need to purge the poison from my system. I'm tiring far too easily. Once I'm back to full strength we'll lure it out into the open and kill it."

"Sounds good to me. How do you propose we do that?"

"It talks to itself, I heard it. He has ultimate faith that the poison will bring me down. He also believes that by eating my heart he'll become much stronger than he is. He'll be watching us. I'll feed as necessary and as opportunity allows, but I'll feign weakness. Once we're ready, you'll wander off and I'll falter. When he comes for me we both take him down."

"So, what happens if he can resurrect as we do?"

"We'll spread the body parts out a bit, leave some in the forest, and carry some with us to be disposed of far, far, away. Actually, as soon as we can contact the king I'll get his thoughts on it."

"Sounds good to me. Let's get in out of the sun now, you need to rest."

"And you need more food, Torvil. I'm still strong enough to defend myself, especially in these rocks where he can't get at me from behind. You go on, feed. I'll be fine." He shimmered into the bear.

"Torvil." The bear stopped and looked at her. "Watch your back, my brother. Watch your back." The bear grunted and ambled away. The bird perched in a tree where it could watch Marlene's hiding place.

THE DAY PASSED AND the king paced. Each time he looked to Tommy the poor guy shook his head sadly. Finally, Sally joined him in the great hall. "I've done another reading. She's been bitten by the snake, but has managed to drive him off for the moment. She been feeding and slowly regaining her strength, but the poison is still weakening her.

"The bear is caring for her and defending her. They plan to find a way to kill it, but I'm not so sure they can. At any rate they're still on the move toward us, she's getting blood and regaining strength.

"Marlene managed to hurt that thing and it's being cautious now. It's learned to respect her, and to fear her, but it's more determined than ever to kill her and eat her heart to gain her strength."

"Can we get help to her, Tommy?"

"Not easily, Sire. I can't get a location on her until we get the phone connection re-established. I still don't have all my electronics up ..."

"Relax, Tommy. I understand. Keep at it, do the best you can. For now we'll have to accept that she and her new ally can handle the situation."

"There's something else," said Sally.

The king arched an eyebrow at her. "Something else?"

"Yes, there's a hawk following them, watching everything, but I have no idea why. It hasn't tried to interfere. I get the sense it's friendly but frightened for some reason."

The king just nodded, and she headed back to her rooms.

Hunting the Hunter

The area was perfect for an ambush. Marlene sighed and let her shoulders slump. The bear was nowhere to be seen. She could feel the snake man nearby, but she could also pick up on his hesitation. He sensed the trap, or he was still wounded. Either way he wasn't taking the bait, and the day was fading.

It had been a few days since her last feeding, and she could feel the effects of the poison once again. If she could get another full feeding before she weakened too much she might be able to beat it, but if she went too long without blood then the poison would weaken her too much.

If they could just manage to kill the snake, then she could relax and allow herself to rest and heal fully. And there was another problem. Their clothes were getting tattered, that would have to be addressed soon as well. It wasn't going to be easy, not one damn bit of it. It had been days since they'd seen another hiker, and weeks since a woman close to her size had happened along.

She sensed the snake withdrawing and whistled. The huge bear soon shambled from the trees and joined her. "Did you get enough to eat?"

"I did," he replied as he shimmered back into human form. "No luck with the snake?"

"He's being wary, holding back. Either he's afraid of a trap, or I hurt him worse than I thought."

"That could be either a good thing or a bad thing. If we can't bait him out, what's our other options?"

116

"We could lead him close to the new castle and let the king deal with him. It wouldn't take the wolves long to ferret him out, and Mother could put him down in a heartbeat."

"She really that tough?"

"You have no idea. Whatever you do, do not piss her off. She's over a million years old and changes into the full saber-toothed tiger. Ella is all grace and good manners until someone rubs her fur the wrong way, then run for cover."

Torvil grinned at her. "Wishing she were here?"

Marlene nodded and sighed. "Yeah, Mother or the king."

"Tell me about him."

"He's a bit younger than Mobutu, but he's a warrior, never doubt that. He fought Mobutu to a standstill at hand to hand. When next they fought the king had a sword in his hand. Give Harald a sword and he's unstoppable."

"All right, maybe that's our best option then. I'm certain either one of us can take the snake man, but the trick seems to be to get close enough. Maybe that wolf pack isn't a bad idea at that. If they could flush him out where I could get at him ..."

"If we ever get to a place where I can get cell reception I'll ask Harald what he wants us to do. Right now I'd kill for somebody to eat." That remark brought a great bellow of laughter from Torvil. "Oh, you think that's funny, do you?"

"Oh gods, girl, yes I do."

"You won't think it's so funny if I have to bite your ass to survive," she grumbled. "Come on, let's see if there's a shelter on the other side of that ridge."

They took their time climbing and it was dark when they reached the top. They no sooner reached the crest when her phone rang. Snatching it from her pocket she answered.

"Harald?"

"Miss Marlene, it's Tommy. Please stay on the line and I'll get the king."

It only took a moment and he was there. "Marlene, are you all right?"

"Barely. Harald we've encountered another non-human. He's part snake or something and his bite is poisonous."

"Yes, Sally saw him in a vision. We've been trying to locate you. Were you bitten?"

"I was. The poison is swift and deadly. However, I managed to wound him in that fight. I was done for, dying and looking forward to reviving to face the death by poison again, that is, if I managed to revive."

"What happened?"

"Torvil found me. He'd been gone, foraging for food, when I got attacked. He fed me enough of his own blood to keep me alive until we encountered a group of hikers and I managed to get a full feeding. That stopped most of the poison, but I feel it growing stronger again."

"You need to feed."

"I do. Harald, I believe if I can get another full feeding I can eradicate the poison from my system. However, there are problems. I need human blood and there's not a lot of them around, and we've still got that snake hunting us. He's keeping his distance for now, but he's staying on our trail."

"Can you defeat him?"

"Yes, if I can feed myself. Torvil could defeat him as well, but the trick is to catch him. We've been trying to lure him out for days, but he won't go for the bait."

"What's your next move?"

"I'm wide open to suggestions."

"Can you trust Torvil to defend you?"

"Absolutely." That brought a grunt and a gentle hip rub from the bear.

"Good. Marlene, feed yourself, be wary, but come home at your own pace. Stay in touch and as soon as possible I'll get help to you."

"Harald, if you send the wolves, tell them to be doubly careful of this thing. It's as fast and strong as a vampire, and for them its bite would be fatal."

"I understand. Marlene, be careful, I don't want to lose you. Sally said something about a hawk as well."

"Yes, there's been a hawk shadowing us for a while now, I have no idea why or what the hell that's all about. It hasn't tried to interfere.

"I'll be careful, I promise. Harald."

"Yes?"

"You owe me big time for this one." She grinned as she returned the phone to her pocket.

"Come on, brother bear, I think I smell smoke. Could be a shelter full of dinner nearby."

He grunted in reply as he followed her off the ridge. They traveled easily in the soft moonlight. As they neared the shelter they heard a scream, a shriek, then something bolted past them. Marlene ducked out of the way and the bear took a swipe at it. Blood sprayed into the air accompanied by another howl of pain, but the creature was too fast for the bear to catch.

Marlene stepped into the shelter to see a woman cowering against the back wall. "Oh Jesus, are you human?" asked the woman. "Quick, get back here. There's something out there. I thought it was a man, but it hissed like a snake and tried to bite me."

"Were you bitten?"

"No, I got it with the bear spray before it could bite me. I ..." She got no further as the vampire struck, her fangs biting deep, and drinking greedily of the hot spurting blood.

Marlene forced herself to release the woman who sank to the ground looking past her shoulder. Weakly she tried to raise her weapon again. "Bear," she gasped.

"I know, he's a friend," said Marlene, as she relieved the woman of the bear spray. "Be still now and rest."

"Are you going to kill me?"

"No, I won't, but that thing out there might. Rest now and let me think."

The woman gasped as the bear entered the shelter and shimmered into a caveman. She swallowed hard and remained very still.

"So, top up your tank?" asked Torvil.

"Yes, she's strong and healthy. I'm able to beat the poison back now. One more good feeding and I should be free of it. Did you get him?"

"No, damned weasel got away again, but I bloodied him up a bit. He was already hurting from the beating you gave him. Now he'll be more dangerous than ever. We'll need to be on our guard."

"Agreed."

"So, what are we going to do with this one?"

"Well, that's a bit of a problem. She fed me well, and now she's weak from loss of blood. If we leave her here that damned snake will get her."

Marlene turned to the terrified woman. "No, girl, you're not caught in the Twilight Zone. I need you to stay with me now, to focus. Where is the nearest town?"

"I passed a town about three days ago."

"I assume you cover a lot of ground every day?"

"Yes. I only have a couple of weeks before I have to go back to work, so I hike fast. What are you going to do with me?"

"We'll take you with us until we get close to the town where you'll be safe from that monster. We'll protect you until then."

"Okay, but aren't you afraid I'll tell people about you?"

"About me?"

"You're a vampire, you drank my blood, and he's ... he's ..., I don't have any idea what the hell he is."

"Torvil's a were-bear," grinned Marlene. "Look, I'm sorry we've messed up your vacation, and you truly did save my life, so we'll protect you and get you back to civilization. Sadly, when we get close I'll have to make you forget all about us and the snake man. You'll just think you got sick on the trail."

"If they take me to a hospital won't they be able to tell you bit me?"

"No, and you won't have a tooth mark to show them."

The woman just sat, thinking. Marlene was slightly bemused. "I have to say, you're taking this all rather well. Most people are a babbling mess by this point."

She sighed and leaned back. "I was twelve when I was raped by my uncle. That hurt a hell of a lot worse than your bite, and you didn't kill me. That other one would have, I know it."

"Yes, he would have."

"Then I guess I should be grateful to you for saving my life. Are you going to feed off me again?"

"No girl, I took all from you I dare to. You need enough strength to carry you back to town. You rest now. We'll keep watch so that thing won't get near you again tonight."

A short while later Torvil noticed the woman staring at him. "What's on your mind?"

"You are," she replied. "I've seen bears like that, and men like you before, but ..."

"In a museum of natural history?" he grinned.

"Yes. Can you tell me?"

"The bear is a cave bear and I'm a Neanderthal/homo sapien hybrid. My mother and father were a mixed marriage." Marlene snickered at that and the woman smiled.

"Please don't make me forget you crazy people. I swear I'll never tell a living soul about you."

Marlene arched an eyebrow at her. "All right, I'll confess. I'm a writer of historical romance. I have lots of vampires in my books, but I'll bet I get it all wrong."

"Everybody does," sighed Marlene. "What's your name?"

"Lilly Reilly."

"Never heard of you."

"I'm not surprised. I'm not famous, but I make a living. Can I ask you something?"

"Sure."

"Are there any were-wolves?"

Marlene chuckled at that. "Yes, there are lots of them. Listen you, are you planning to pick my brain for writing material all the way back to town?"

"Oh god yes. I swear I'll never tell a single person about you, but I could go for years with some of what you ..."

Marlene just shook her head at the bright eyed eager young woman. "Torvil, what am I going to do with this one?"

"If it were up to me, I'd let her keep her memory. After all, if I'm going into hiding for a few centuries I'll need something good to read."

Marlene sighed elaborately and rolled her eyes. "Oh, may the gods help me. Both of you get some sleep, I'll take the watch."

WHILE MARLENE WAS MULLING it over, the king was facing another problem. He'd just been warned by Bill Walker that a police car was headed for the castle. Terry Sawchuk came into the great hall to hear the king muttering about nosy cops.

"What's up, Boss?"

"Huh? Oh, Terry, it's just a police car headed for the castle, at this hour of the night. I don't like it, but since I have no idea what's going on, I ..."

"Let me deal with it, Sire," grinned Terry. "Just stall the bugger until I can get a suit on. Be right back."

He hurried away and Harald grinned. He had come to trust Terry Sawchuk, and to admire the man's tenacity and resourcefulness. Suddenly the alarms sounded, and Harald's grin widened as he listened to the new butler respond to the intercom.

"Eldredsson residence. The hour is late, and Mr. Eldredsson is not receiving. Whoever you are I suggest you depart then make an appointment."

"Listen, you snot-nosed limy bastard, this is the sheriff. Now you open that damned gate."

The butler looked to Harald who shook his head. "I will not unless you have a warrant. Do you indeed have such a warrant? If not then I strongly suggest you get one before you return. Good night, Sir."

"Well done," grinned Harald.

The intercom began buzzing immediately. The butler looked to the king, but Terry had just returned. "I'll just deal with that. Tell him I'll meet him outside the door. Oh, stall him for a few minutes first."

He nodded and answered the buzzer again. "Eldredsson residence."

"Listen you limy son of a bitch, you open that damned gate. I don't need a fucking warrant, I have a complaint and probable cause of a crime."

"Very well, remain in your car until the dogs have been called in. Someone will meet you at the front door. Follow the driveway and do not deviate from the path for your own safety."

"Charles, that was perfect," grinned Harald. "Looks like you're on, Terry."

"Want to listen in, Sire?"

"Oh yes, indeed I do." Grinning, Terry tossed him a radio then set out for the main door.

The sheriff was fuming, but still in the car as there were two huge wolves staring at him. Terry stepped through the door and held it open. The wolves disappeared inside. The sheriff got out and approached. He started to speak, but Terry stopped him, flashing a badge in his face. "All right, just what the fuck do you want here?"

"Jesus Christ, is that badge real?"

"Yes it is, now what the hell do you want?"

"Look, I have a complaint ..."

"Some dipshit tried to fly a drone over this area and it got shot down, right?"

"Yes. That drone is ..."

"Destroyed, that's what it is."

"Look, I'm the law around here and I have a right to know what the hell is going on. I..."

"No you don't, Sheriff. Your jurisdiction ends at the highway. What goes on here is classified way the hell above your pay grade. Look up there, see that wall?" Terry reached for his radio. "Sniper one, are you in position?"

"Sniper one responding. I have a shot, do I have a green light?"

"Not just yet. Sniper two?"

"Two here, I have a clear shot, do I have a go?"

"Hold. Sniper three?"

"In position. I have a shot. Orders?"

"Hold. All right, Sheriff, here's how this works. Things, odd things, crazy things, may happen in this area, but we'll deal with any and all of it. Anyone caught snooping around will disappear forever. Am I making myself perfectly clear?"

The sheriff was visibly shaken. He swallowed hard then replied. "Perfectly clear."

"So, was it your son or brother who lost the drone?"

"Brother-in-law," sighed the sheriff, his shoulders sagging.

"He got a name?"

"What? why?"

"I want his computer and any footage he may have gained before we shot down the drone. I'll also want to question him personally."

"Now wait, is that completely necessary? Look, I'll talk to him, confiscate any and all evidence he may have gathered, and bring it to you. Just don't drag him in or my life will be hell for months."

Terry gave him a hard look then relented. "All right, Sheriff. You can deliver the evidence to the farmer who lives just down by the highway. And Sheriff, don't come back here again, clear?"

"Very clear," replied the sheriff as he climbed back into his car.

Terry watched him go until he went through and the gate closed behind him. He reached for his radio. "Eric, Jimmy, Vassily, good job guys, we're clear." One of the snipers waved and Terry went back inside.

"Olla, Igor, great job. You scared the crap out of him."

"As did you, Terry," grinned Olla. "Tough government agent."

Harald was chuckling as Terry returned. "Terry, that was wonderful. I doubt he'll ever come back here again. How did you know it was a family member who owned the drone?"

"Just a guess, Sire. In truth, I expect it was the Sheriff himself who owned that machine. He showed up here late to throw a scare into us, and that tells me he didn't get a damn thing before Eric shot down the spy."

"You believe it was he who flew the drone?"

"Oh yeah, notice how fast his story and attitude changed when I said I wanted to interview the owner? Yes sir, that was his drone all right. Now he'll try to go over my head, but all he'll get is a denial of my existence."

"Terry, you're a treasure and I'm glad you're on my side. Go back to your woman, get some rest, my friend."

He grinned and saluted as he left the great hall. The king relaxed back in his chair, still smiling.

Love and Death in the Forest

They'd traveled for two days with Lilly constantly asking questions. She'd gathered far more information about them than Marlene would have liked, but for some reason she hadn't made a fuss about it. The night was dark and they'd occupied a shelter so they could have fire to keep Lilly warm.

"Marlene, can you tell me about how you became a vampire? You know, what led you to it, how ..."

"No." That answer left no room for argument. "Mother once trusted her stories to another, a woman. The woman in turn twisted the tales and told them to her son, Bram Stoker. When Mother realized what had happened it was too late to stop it. Now we have all this stupid shit out there about vampires.

"Ask me one more question and it'll be the last."

Lilly shrank from the fury in the vampire's eyes. She slowly moved over closer to Torvil who patted her knee reassuringly. "You'll need to feed again soon, little sister. You're getting seriously cranky."

She rounded on him with the fury close to the surface, but she beat it down. Marlene shuddered with the effort to retain control. Finally she spoke. "It's the damned poison, I can feel it still trying to gain control, to weaken me.

"Lilly, a vampire lives every moment of her life with the killing lust near the surface. We beat it down, learn to control it, and most of the time it recedes into the background. However, some are made vampire

126

who can't get that control, or lose their power over it, give in to the mad killing lust, the burning thirst for blood.

"One of those made me what I am. Fortunately, Mother was there to help me as I learned control, and then the king taught me to hunt. I can't tell you these things and leave your memories intact. Mother's mistake proves that.

"I'm wounded and close to the edge now, stop pushing me, for your own sake, you have to stop."

The girl swallowed hard and met Marlene's eyes. She saw the pleading there as well as the rage boiling just beneath the surface. "Marlene, I'm sorry, I am. I swear I'll never tell a soul anything, and I won't write anything either. I don't want to hurt you, and I don't want to use you. You fascinate me, I want to know all about you, and ..."

She stopped speaking and blushed. Marlene gazed into her eyes and saw the fear and pleading there as well as something else. Lust. She sighed and let her shoulders slump. "Are you kidding me? Now? I'm here fading from poison, smelling like a goat or worse, and trying not to drink you dry, and you're getting lusty?"

Lilly's face was flame red at this point and she couldn't make eye contact. "I can't help it."

"Mother of Mercy, Torvil, what am I going to do with this one?"

"Oh no, I'm not getting mixed up in this," he grinned. "We're close enough to the town. You go on ahead and feed yourself. Really top up your tank, then come back to us. I'll keep her safe until you get back."

"You promise?" Marlene's eyes were still locked on Lilly.

"Cross my heart," he grinned.

Marlene shook a finger at the wide-eyed girl then slipped out of the shelter and into the darkness. She didn't head for the town though. The hawk was perched in a tree, staring at a clump of bushes. Marlene vanished into the night and waited with the patience of the tiger that was part of her. It wasn't a long wait. She soon heard LeBlanc's soft whispers.

"So, the blood drinker goes away to feed, Cher. Now we kills Mr. Bear. No bear, no protection for the blood drinker."

LeBlanc suddenly appeared in the entrance to the shelter. Torvil had no chance to change into the bear, but it wasn't necessary. Marlene slammed into LeBlanc from behind knocking him to the ground with her on his back. He fought wildly, but couldn't dislodge her. As strong arms tightened around his neck and powerful legs squeezed the air from his lungs he knew he was going to die.

"Go ahead, Blood Drinker, bite LeBlanc. Drink his blood."

"I don't feed from vermin," she snarled, as she gave a mighty twist and his neck snapped. She released him and watched until the body stopped twitching. Torvil grabbed the body and dragged it outside then hurled it into the woods.

"Keep an eye on that," said Marlene, as he returned. "If it comes back to life, kill it."

Torvil nodded. "Count on it."

With that Marlene took another glance at Lilly who was cowering in fear. "I'll be back for you," she said, as she vanished into the night once again.

"Is she going to kill me, too?" asked Lilly.

"I doubt that," grinned Torvil. "If she was planning to kill you it would have happened already. I think she likes you."

"Truly? You really think so?"

"Yup."

"Why? I mean, what makes you say that?"

"She didn't leave before, but stayed to see if the snake man was nearby. If she didn't like you she'd have been long gone."

"Maybe she stayed for you."

"Oh, I'm sure that was part of it all right, but she knows I can handle myself. Even if I'm killed she knows I'll come back. No girl, she hung around to make certain you were safe. She likes you, no doubt about it."

"Yeah, well, she scared the hell out of me earlier. All I did was ask a question."

"Normally that wouldn't make a difference, but she's hungry and the poison from the snake man's bite is dragging her down. The hunger for blood is powerful at a time like this. As she tells it, it's an all-consuming thirst, driving all else from the mind except the need for blood and the desire to kill. When she's hungry she needs to stay totally focused to overcome the killing lust, the burning hunger."

"Wow, and I was distracting her. Shit. What should I do?"

Torvil grinned. "Relax. When she gets back you'll see a very different Marlene. Oh, don't mistake me, the girl is a cold-blooded killer, but she's also a good and loyal friend. You've just had a peek at the darker side of her nature. Once she's well fed and free of the poison you'll see a more human side of her."

"I sure hope so."

"Can't get her out of your mind, can you?"

"No, I can't, and I don't know why. I've only felt like this once before. I made a complete fool of myself, and the rejection drove me into a depression that was almost lethal. I tried suicide and failed. The councilor suggested I write to distract myself, and damned if I wasn't good at it. I've been a reclusive writer ever since, for the past five years."

Torvil was smiling at her and she was completely relaxed with him. "So tell me, what happened?"

"That's hard to explain. First that thing attacked and I hit it with the bear spray, then suddenly she was there. I didn't even see her face. Darn good thing too, her vampire face is scary as hell."

"I second that," he grinned. "Go on."

"Well, she just swept me into her arms and bit me. I was already in shock, I'm sure, but she held me so gently. It was more like a lovers embrace than an attack. When she stopped it was like a piece of me was suddenly gone.

"God, I'm so pathetic. I'd sell my soul to be held in her arms like that again. Are you sure she likes me?"

"Positive. Girl, you've got a serious crush going on there."

"Pretty sad, huh."

"Oh I don't know. I've been like that a few times. It feels pretty good as I recall."

"Oh yeah, when was the last time you had a crush going?"

"About seventy-five years ago, roughly speaking."

"So, what happened? Did you ever get a date with her?"

"We were married until this year when she was murdered. I went crazy all over the men who hurt her, and that's what sent Marlene after me."

"What do you mean?"

"Apparently, the vampire king doesn't want humans to know about the existence of us non-humans. My killing spree was drawing too much attention. Marlene was sent to bring me in or dispose of me. She talked me into coming with her. That brings us to you."

"Wait until she gets back, and then see how things stand. I think she likes you."

"Wish I could be so sure of that."

"You can, girl. Twice now she's asked me what she's going to do with you. Believe me when I say, if she didn't like you, she wouldn't ask."

"She'd just kill me?"

"That or leave you on the trail with no memory. Relax, be patient, see how it goes."

Lilly nodded thoughtfully. She settled down by the fire and Torvil went out to check on the snake man's body. It was starting to move. He went into bear mode and tore it apart, scattering the pieces around in the trees.

Once back at the shelter he resumed human form and struggled into his ragged clothes. "Let's see that damned abomination come back from that," he grumbled. Shuddering, Lilly pretended to be asleep.

IT WAS LATE, AND TWO men staggered from the bar singing a bawdy song. As they made their way down the street a girl was suddenly between them, singing along. One man grabbed her ass, and she nuzzled his neck. He gasped as her fangs bit deep and his blood flowed into her mouth. She drank as much as she dared then released him.

Their companion had continued singing and she joined back in. With her urging, the man she'd bitten picked up the song as he staggered and leaned against her. She then nuzzled his companion who suddenly stopped singing. When she finished with him she steered them into some bushes and left them there.

A short time later two teenagers who were necking under a large tree suddenly began to argue. The girl angrily stormed away, but her boyfriend couldn't follow. He tried to get to his feet, but something grabbed him from behind and, with a startled squawk, he was pulled back, a hand clamped over his mouth and sharp fangs buried in his neck.

The girl looked back to see her lover in the arms of another woman. "You fucking bastard, I fucking hate you," she screamed. She turned and, with tears streaming down her face, ran away.

A harsh voice spoke as the vampire released her victim. *"Go home and sleep. You fought with your girlfriend. You remember nothing more than that. Go."* He staggered to his feet, and with shaky steps, headed home. A few moments later a homeless man donated more blood to her need, then she set out for the trail and the shelter. She felt she was free of the poison at last.

LILLY AWAKENED ALONE in the shelter. She could hear the soft voices of Torvil and Marlene outside. She smiled as she listened. "Are you certain he's dead?"

"Can't be certain of anything with this one, but I tore him apart and spread him around a bit. If he comes back from that it'll take him a while. What do you want to do here?"

"I want to make sure Lilly is safe, then I want us to cover some distance. I want to get this mission finish, report to the king, then have a week long bath."

"You sure that's all you want?"

"Torvil, if you start teasing me about Lilly, I swear I'll bite your ass."

He chuckled at that, then sobered. "You scared the hell out of her yesterday, little sister. She's tough and can take it, but if you really like this girl, you might want to let her know."

"Is that the voice of experience talking?"

"That it is. Now, you may be well fed, but this old bear's hungry. Go take your girl home then we'll meet up on the trail." With that he stripped off, changed into the bear, and ambled away into the forest.

Marlene gathered his clothes and stowed them into the backpack. She tossed it into the shelter and followed it in. Lilly was there, gazing up at her hopefully. "Oh stop with the puppy dog eyes." Marlene sighed and sat beside her. She could feel the girl's fear as well as her attraction, and she was getting lost in those big brown eyes.

"I scared you yesterday, didn't I?" She just nodded. "That's what life's like around a vampire, scary, dangerous, unpredictable." Again Lilly nodded. "Come here." Marlene gathered the frightened girl into her arms and sighed.

"Marlene?" asked a soft voice from her shoulder. "Are you okay?"

"No, I'm not. You have to stop this right now."

"Stop what?"

"Feeling so damn good in my arms."

"Is that really such a bad thing?"

"Right now, it is. Lilly, I'm on a mission, a dangerous mission. I need to get Torvil safely back to the king, I have no idea how many humans and dogs are hunting us, I have no idea if that snake-man is truly dead, and I can't have you distracting me when I need to be focused."

"So, do you really find me distracting?"

Marlene looked down and saw a bright smile below those large liquid eyes. Lilly began to bat her eyes and Marlene howled with laughter and hugged her tightly. "Yes, you terrible brat, I do find you distracting."

"But being distracted at the wrong time, or trying to protect me when you need to focus elsewhere could be fatal. I get it, but I can't seem to help myself. Please, Marlene, don't make me forget you, please."

"I won't make you forget, girl, I won't. But I do have to let you go for a while until I get this mission finished. Once I'm free of this I'll come for you, Miss Lilly Reilly of the devastating eyes."

"You promise?"

"Lilly, stop and think, is this truly what you want? Do you have any idea at all what life with me would be like?"

"You mean terribly exciting and scary as hell?"

"Yes, that," chuckled Marlene.

Lilly just snuggled deeper into Marlene's embrace. "I can't help myself; you fascinate me. You scare the bejeebers out of me, but you attract me as well, and I can't stop thinking about you."

Marlene gazed into her eyes, but didn't speak. Lilly closed her eyes and raised her lips for a kiss, but Marlene pulled away. Tears suddenly flowed from those eyes and Lilly tried to disentangle herself from Marlene's arms.

Marlene was having none of that. "Come back here and let me hold you."

"Marlene?"

"Woman, if I kiss you now I'm not likely to ever let you out of my sight for a hundred years or more. I can't do this right now, I don't dare. I have to finish the mission. Now, look me in the eye and tell me you're completely certain."

"I'm certain," she breathed softly. "I'm in love with you, Marlene the Vampire. I know I'm a fool, and doomed, but I can't help myself."

"I can't either, Lilly, my sweet. Listen to me now. I'm going to take you back to that town. Can you get home from there?" Lilly nodded. "All right, then you write down the address for me. As soon as I'm free to do so, I'll come to you. If you're still certain then, I'll spirit you away and keep you forever."

"Oh god, Marlene, you promise?"

"I swear it, Lilly. Oh, and that's Marlene de France, not Marlene the Vampire."

"Right, got it," giggled Lilly. "Marlene?"

"Hmm?"

"Can I stay right here in your arms for a few more minutes before you take me back?"

Marlene gently tightened her arms around the girl's shoulders and kissed the top of her head. "Yes you can, sweet girl, yes you can."

An hour later Lilly was in the town waiting for a bus and Marlene was on the trail again. The day was cool and cloudy so she set out at an easy jog with the hawk following high above. Torvil's scent said he was ahead of her.

WHILE MARLENE WAS SAYING goodbye to Lilly, consciousness returned to LeBlanc. Once again he became aware of himself and his surroundings. He tried to move and the horror of his situation began to set in, his body had been dismembered. Fighting down the terror, he began to focus his will, and far away in the new lair, the queen of vampires awakened screaming.

"Sally, Sally my love, hush now, I've got you. Nothing can harm you now. Hush, sweet Sally, it was only a dream. Hush now."

Trembling, she cuddled deeper into his embrace. "Oh dear gods, Harald. We need to warn Marlene."

"What is it, Sally?"

"They killed it, Harald, Marlene killed the snake man, but he started to revive. The bear then killed him again and dismembered the body, scattering the pieces around. Harald, it's reviving. I felt the power as it realized what had happened and began to call to its body. It seems to have some sort of telekinetic ability, at least where its body parts are concerned. We have to warn her."

"And we will do that and more, my love, as soon as you get some tea and toast to settle your nerves. Come, let's head to the kitchen and see if our Elaine has beaten us to it."

They arrived to find the young woman smiling as she set tea and toast for one on the table. "It appears I'm not the only psychic one in this household," smiled Sally. "Harald, you go on. I'll join you in the great hall as soon as I settle myself and get dressed." He kissed the top of her head and left her to her tea.

Harald strode into the great hall like a man with a mission. Several people were already gathered there as the day was well along. "Tommy, report, are all your instruments up and running?"

"Yes, Sire, that and more. I'm adding a few of my personal inventions. Forgive me Sire, but you seem to have something specific on your mind."

"I have. I have further information about the snake-man hunting Marlene. It can return from the lands beyond just we do, moreover, even though the bear has dismembered it, it can pull itself back together."

This brought a round of laughter from the assembled folks and Harald had to grin himself. "Yes, well, I guess that did sound a bit funny, however, according to Sally, it's true. She might be wrong about that, but I doubt it."

"I wouldn't bet against it either," agreed Terry Sawchuk. "Boss, I've been doing some digging, and I may have something here."

"Tell me."

"Sire, when you first spoke of this I started to put out a few feelers. Once Tommy told me it called itself LeBlanc I focused my inquiries on the back bayou country. There's a man named LeBlanc, a professional hunter, and all round mystery man.

"Here's what I've got on him so far. He's about average size, talks to himself a lot, is suspected of several murders, is a deadly and extremely successful hunter, tenacious, savage fighter, reputed to hunt his own food and eat it raw. His nickname is Cottonmouth.

"Now, if this is our guy, his venom will play holy hell with the blood. It's not fatal in and of itself, but it will incapacitate the victim quickly. It can cause a host of issues including the loss of body control.

"On the bright side, there is an antivenin. I've taken the liberty of acquiring a supply for us in case we need it."

"Well done, Terry, well done. I don't suppose you know why that thing is so far from its home?"

"He's a professional hunter, Sire. Someone hired him. It seems some land grabber met his fate in a tangle with a bear a while ago, and his brother didn't like it. He hired LeBlanc to find and kill the bear. I'm betting it was Marlene who made the kill since he's so fixated on her."

"You're probably right about that. Now, we have to get some help to Marlene."

"We should go," said Illya.

"No, my friend. Autumn is upon us, and hunting seasons are open. There are far too many fools with rifles in the forest now. They'd shoot the wolves for sport. Besides, this creature is as fast and strong as a vampire. I'll go myself."

"Forgive me, Sire," spoke up a small man, "but I don't think that's the best idea."

"Talk to me, Clyde," said Harald.

"Well, Sire, you said you needed something to build Marlene's confidence, to help her become more mature in her thinking. If you go bail her out ..."

"I could undermine her confidence, or at least make it look that way to her," sighed the king.

"Let me go, Sire," grinned a tall man in a military style uniform.

"Jimmy?"

"I won't try to engage the enemy, Sir. They've each brought it down, so we know they can handle it. The issue seems to be the venom. If I meet them on the trail with a few doses of the antivenin, that wouldn't seem like a bail out, just a supply drop."

"Jimmy could also drop off a SAT phone so they'd always be in contact," added Tommy.

"All right. Are you sure you can find them, Jimmy?" asked the king.

"That's my buddy's job," he grinned. "How about it, Igor? You up for a few days hiking in the fresh air?"

"Me?" exclaimed the youth. "Oh hell yeah, I'm up for it. Can I go, Grandpa?"

"You stay out of trouble and do as Mr. Jimmy says. Watch out for snakes."

"Go pack," grinned Jimmy. "We're traveling in human form. Well, you may have to go wolf once or twice to catch a scent, but that's all. Don't worry, Sire, I'll be carrying weapons as well. I'll keep him safe."

"And by sending a human and a youth to bring the antivenin it doesn't undermine her belief in my confidence in her. All right, but Jimmy, be extremely careful."

"Understood, Sire," replied Jimmy. "Tommy, best guess, where are they?"

Tommy brought up a map on the big screen. "My best guess is right about here. Marlene called in from here yesterday."

Jimmy gazed at the map for a moment. "All right, here's our insertion point. We should be well ahead of them, but connect in a day or two at the most. Sire, I could pull them out at the insertion point."

"That will be Marlene's call, Jimmy. It's her mission, let her make that decision. Just tell her not to waste too much time on that snake-man. Tell her to lead him close and we'll deal with him from this end."

"Understood. Come on, Igor. Let's gather our gear, steal Eric's jeep, and then hit the road."

As they left the hall the king turned back to Illya. "I'm curious, my friend, why did you let the boy go?"

"He survived Stephan Krebs' death camp as leader of their pack. He grows stronger each day, and Queen Sally tells me he will one day be the alpha of his own pack. He needs to gain experience in this world if he is to lead his people successfully. For some reason he looks to Mr. Tommy and to Mr. Jimmy as role models. They can teach him the things I cannot."

"Being the king isn't always fun and games, is it?"

"No, Sire. Some days being the Alpha is the hardest task of all."

Harald nodded then turned to Tommy. "Tommy, you spoke of inventions. Is there any magic you'd care to share with me?"

Grinning, Tommy called up a map of the state on the big screen. "Your map seems to be missing a piece, Tommy."

"Indeed, Sire. Watch. This is a satellite view of the area. With this map I, or anyone with a computer, can look down into the back yard of any house they choose." So saying he zeroed in on a house. The scene moved closer until distinct features of the property could be seen. He even identified the make and model of the family car.

"Anyone with a computer can do this? Forgive me, Tommy, but I find this technology disturbing."

"Keep watching, Sire. I will now try to zoom in on us." As the view began to move closer to their castle the screen suddenly went all fuzzy and then blank."

"What happened, Tommy?"

"My new scattering field is broadcasting twenty-four hours a day now, Sire. There will be nobody peering over our shoulder. The same thing will happen to any drones that fly by, cameras will be affected as well, unless they are old fashioned film cameras."

Harald chuckled softly and patted Tommy on the shoulder. "This is why you're the official court sorcerer, Tommy. Well done, my friend.

"Ah, here's Sally. We appear to have things well in hand, my sweet. Your warning has been taken to heart and help is already on the way to Marlene. Terry has determined who and what the snake man is, and Jimmy is on the way to deliver the antivenin to Marlene."

"That's wonderful. Did you figure out the last part?"

"Last part?"

"How to kill that thing and make it stay dead."

"No," he sighed as he resumed his chair. "That's still a work in progress. Do you have anything more about the hawk?"

"It's still watching. I get the sense it's afraid of the snake man, but still watching him anyway. It also seems to want something from the bear, but I have no idea what."

THE PAIN WAS INTENSE, but LeBlanc fought his way through it by talking to himself as he chewed thoughtfully. "That was close, Cher, too close. Mr. Bear, he has sharp claws. Hurt our eyes, she did. Bear spray. Woman has venom too, Cher. Then the blood drinker catch us, Cher. Killed us. Ha, we come back as always, Cher.

"Poor Mr. Deer, lucky LeBlanc find you. Need you for healing. Time and meat, heal hurts, then hunt again."

LeBlanc slept beside the deer carcass for nearly two days before he rose ready for the hunt again. He wasn't fully healed, but he could function. He wasn't hunting Marlene now, he had more immediate needs. Two groups of hikers passed his hiding place until he saw what he wanted, a lone male hiker about his size.

The man had no chance as he was struck from behind. A body slammed into him, fangs bit into his shoulder, and a stone crashed into his skull killing him instantly. LeBlanc dragged the victim off the trail and into the woods. Swiftly he stripped it bare and dressed in its clothes.

He smashed the man's phone then dragged the body to a steep drop off and threw the body over the edge. "That will do, Cher." With that he set out for the trail and the town he sensed nearby. Once in town he slipped into the shadows to wait for nightfall.

In the darkness he hunted, passing house after house until he found one empty. A swift search soon turned up the spare key under a flower pot. He slipped inside and began to explore. A short time later he left the house, a new rifle clutched tightly in his hands.

He patted the weapon affectionately as he returned to the hiking trail. "Now for you, blood drinker. My new friend wants you, Cher, he does. For you and brother bear. Two of you and now two of us, right Cher? Two on two is a better fight, yeah?" He caught the scent, it was a couple of days old, but he was on the trail once again.

Even as he hunted he could feel the eyes of the bird on him.

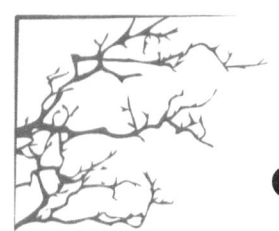

Closer to Home

Days passed and LeBlanc was getting frustrated. They were moving faster now, and he was struggling to catch up. They were sticking to the trail so that part was easy enough, but he'd been spotted by other hikers and reported for hunting on the trail. Several times he'd had to hide from the lawmen who were searching for him.

With a snarl of impatience, so rare for him, LeBlanc set out at a run. Even as darkness fell, he ran on. Well into the next day he noticed the scent getting stronger. "At last, we gain ground, Cher. Soon we will have the blood drinker."

Even as LeBlanc began to celebrate catching up, Marlene had a visitor on the trail. She spotted the two hikers moving towards her and signaled Torvil to stay back out of sight. As the hikers drew nearer she let out a laugh of joy. "Jimmy, Igor, what are you two doing here?"

"We brought you gifts," grinned Igor, as he jogged up to her.

"Gifts?"

"First this," said Jimmy, passing her a small case.

"What is it, Jimmy?"

"Antitoxin for the snake bite. Terry learned who and what your snake probably is, and we got you some antidote."

"Sweet. I thought I'd beaten it, but I'm getting tired, and I can feel it still in my system."

"Here, let me give you a shot right now. You'll have five more doses with you in this case. The king says to not waste any time with this thing, but get home as fast as you can. Do you want me to arrange an extraction?"

141

"No. I don't want to take a chance of Torvil being spotted close to the new castle. We'll come home the back way. Besides, I don't want to lead that snake anywhere near the new lair."

"King Harald says not to worry about that, Miss Marlene," said Igor. "He says to let it follow you and the others will deal with it."

She nodded slowly. "All right, we'll pick up the pace, but we'll keep an eye out, and if it gets close enough ..."

"It's already close," replied the youth. "I smell something evil on the wind, and I feel a wrongness about this place. That hawk is looking at something in that thicket. Perhaps I could ..."

"No, I like you, Igor. I don't want to lose my buddy so young. Igor, I know you're a warrior to be reckoned with already, but this thing is horribly fast and dangerous. Go back to the castle and tell the king we're coming. Tell him we killed the snake, but even though we spread the body parts around quite a bit it still revived."

"He knows," said Jimmy. "The queen has had several visions about this thing. They'll be ready and waiting."

"That's a relief. So, what else have you brought me?"

"Three bottles of the finest," grinned Jimmy, as he passed the backpack to her, "courtesy of Gudrun. Now this is a special phone, works off the satellites. You've always got reception."

"This is amazing, gentlemen. Go now, before that snake catches up with us."

"Too late for that," said Igor. "He's near, but not so near, yet my instincts are... Get down!" He pushed Marlene aside and grabbed Jimmy just as a shot rang out. The boy spun around and, grabbing at his shoulder, began to swear in Russian as he tried to staunch the blood.

Marlene had already shifted onto killing mode and was racing a zig-zag pattern as she bore down on the most likely place for the shot to have come from. Jimmy was bandaging up Igor's shoulder as she met the bear coming the other way. He had a rifle in his jaws. Marlene took the weapon and they hurried back to Jimmy and Igor.

The boy was still muttering in Russian as Torvil shimmered into the man. "Dirty bastard slipped away from me again. I messed him up a bunch, and took his toy, but he escaped me. I'm really working up a serious dislike for that slippery fucker, as you Americans would say."

"Americans? Sorry mate," grinned Jimmy. "I'm a Brit, Igor's Russian, and Miss Marlene is French. No Yanks here unless it's you."

Torvil let out a great bellow of laughter. "No, sir, I'm not even human. So, since nobody is fainting from fright, I suspect you've been sent by the king."

"They brought us presents, Torvil. Jimmy's given me a shot of antivenin and they've brought a couple of bottles of blood. We're getting near enough to the castle now, this should hold me over until we get there."

"Good to know. So, do we dig in and finish that snake before we move on?"

"No, the king says come home. Lead the damned snake close enough and he'll deal with it. We just have to keep it out of sight until he gets there."

"Works for me. Now, I mean no offense, but you two fellas seem to be of a bit more delicate constitution than Marlene and I. We'll just stick around here for a while so you can put some distance between you and the snake."

Jimmy nodded and led Igor back along the trail. Torvil shimmered back into the bear then ambled off the trail. Marlene scooped up the backpack and followed him. She sat beside him, sipping slowly from the bottle. "You know, I have no idea at all what she puts in this stuff to keep it fresh, but it seems to work. I have no idea what the hell that hawk wants either."

Torvil shimmered back into the man. "What happened back there, little sister?"

"That boy's wolf senses are keen; this I can tell you. He sensed the snake, then the danger. He pushed both me and Jimmy out of the way, but he took the bullet. The thing is, I'm willing to bet, in wolf form, he just might be able to defeat that thing."

"He's got courage, I'll say that for him. He can cuss pretty good in Russian too."

"Yes he can," chuckled Marlene. "He doesn't know I can speak Russian, though."

"And you're planning to tell him at the most embarrassing moment possible, right?"

"Oh yes indeed, brother bear. That's exactly what I'm planning. So, I'm feeling better now, what do you think, hunt down LeBlanc or get back on the road?"

"You're the boss, little sister. It's up to you."

"Let's give the boys a few hours more to get well off the trail then we'll head for home. We'll take our time now, so LeBlanc doesn't get lost. Harald now knows what he's dealing with, and he'll be ready."

"What do you think he'll do?"

"I have no idea, but you can bet it'll be nasty, and it'll be permanent. We're having no luck making that bastard stay dead, but Harald will." Just then the new phone rang. "Marlene here."

"Marlene, it's Harald. Jimmy's well away, you can move on now."

"On our way."

"Marlene, be wary, but lead that abomination to me here. I'll deal with it. Oh, I'm afraid I blew your cover."

"Oh?"

"I inadvertently let it slip to Igor that you can swear better than he can in Russian." That brought a howl of laughter from Marlene. "Marlene, be careful, but come home now. The weather is turning colder, especially up where you are."

"All right, Harald, I'd guess we're about a week away, more or less. We'll go slow enough so LeBlanc can keep up, but we'll stay on the move."

Torvil rose and stretched. "We should be on our way. I can smell old snaky close by now. Young Jimmy took his rifle so we don't have that to worry about."

"Right you are, brother bear," said Marlene, as she swept up the backpack and set out. Torvil shimmered into the bear and followed close behind, his ears ever attuned for sounds of pursuit.

The summer had passed into autumn and the bushes were heavily laden with ripe berries. Marlene slowed their pace somewhat so Torvil could eat his fill and thereby keep up his strength. Twice she managed to feed on passing hikers, and she still had one bottle of blood in her pack. She was starting to feel good about the possibility of ending this mission.

She seemed lost in thought and Torvil grinned at her. "Thinking about a big-eyed girl who asks way too many questions?"

"Huh? What? Oh, yeah, I was. That's exactly what I was doing."

"I'd say the snake man wasn't the only thing that bit you," he chuckled.

"Oh?"

"I'd say the love bug got it's fangs into you too."

Marlene sighed. "Sadly, I'd have to agree with you, brother bear. It's been over two hundred years since anyone could get under my skin like this. Strangest part is, it's a woman this time."

"Not your normal choice?"

"Not usually, but seriously, define normal, especially where a non-human is concerned."

"Girl, I always define normal by what feels right. You know girls are my weakness, but over the centuries there were a couple of lads who held my attention. I believe us non-humans to be truly sensual creatures.

"I am curious though, did you leave her memories intact?"

"I did, but I put a compulsion on her to never speak of it aloud, ever."

"Planning to look her up again?"

"Oh hell, yes."

"I truly wish you happiness there, Marlene. I've already warned her about how grouchy you get when you're hungry."

"Oh, gee thanks, Torvil. You're too good to me." Torvil howled with laughter, and she smiled. "Get some sleep, brother bear, then we'll head out again." He nodded then closed his eyes as he settled back.

Dawn came and with it the first heavy frost. Torvil stood up and shook himself. He had changed into the bear in the night to keep warm. "Are you all right, little sister?"

"I'm good," she replied. "We vampires don't feel the cold as much as humans do. Come on, let's cover some ground. I can feel old snaky getting closer.

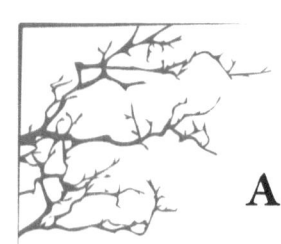

A Different Attack

Next day she caught the scent. Blood. A moment later Marlene found the blood trail and then the mangled body of a hiker. LeBlanc's scent was all over it as well. Fully alert for an ambush, she carefully investigated the body. The man had been bitten then partially eaten.

She snarled as Torvil shimmered into the man right beside her. "It's the snake."

"I know," she replied. "I also know he left the body here for us to find. What I don't understand is why."

"I know why," replied Torvil as he went into bear mode again. He nudged her back towards the trail then set out at a dead run.

Marlene struggled a bit to keep up. The backpack flopping around was holding down her speed and she was getting seriously cranky. Just as she was about to stop, the bear slowed and tested the air. There it was again, the scent of fresh blood ahead of them. Torvil shimmered back into the man, swearing in a language Marlene had never heard before.

"I smell another body," she said as she caught her breath.

"Oh yes, and there will be still more," he replied.

"Torvil, you said you know why he's doing this. Talk to me."

"He's taunting you with the smell of blood, using that to mask his own scent, and he's killing every hiker on the trail to keep you from feeding. Also, the bodies will be found, and the trail will soon be alive with hunters, dogs, and god knows what else."

"Are you serious?"

"I surely am."

147

"God dammit to hell, Torvil, we have to stay out of sight and he's trying to turn this trail into a media circus. What does he hope to gain?"

"We have only one option left, and he knows that," replied Torvil. "We have to get off the trail and deeper into the forest. That will slow us down and make it a lot harder for you to feed. It will also allow him to get a lot closer to us unseen."

"I'm going to find a way to finish this snake man permanently, if it's the last thing I do," she snarled. "Unfortunately, you're right, we have no option here, we have to get off the trail. Keep an eye out while I report in to the king then we'll head for the deep woods. Dammit, I hope we get home before the snows fall, and don't you even think about hibernating on me." He was chuckling as she pulled out the new phone.

WHILE MARLENE MADE her way deeper into the forest, life at the castle was settling into a routine. Battle tactics had resumed under Gudrun's guidance, several more servants were hired, and Tommy's inventive genius was hard at work. The grounds were patrolled night and day by sharp eyed wolves and vampires as well as by the electronic surveillance.

The king was feeling more secure by the day. They now had a butler, three lady's maids, a cook, three grounds keepers, and two field hands to help Bill Walker. In the small town nearby, Harald had also located a blacksmith who was a fair weapons maker. He commissioned a new sword from him.

All through the town the people began to feel the presence of the castle. The servants shopped locally, the gentry, as they came to be called, did as well, and the people felt a new prosperity.

Oddly, even though the rest of the country appeared to be growing more violent, violence in the small town seemed to be on the decrease. The local toughs and troublemakers were suddenly becoming more subdued. Even the sheriff, a bully by nature, became more respectful after a private meeting with the new owner of the castle.

And, if anyone took note of the blacked-out bus that left the castle at night about once each week, then returned the following night, they never spoke of it. The country was going to hell in a hand basket, but their little corner of the world seemed to be escaping the madness.

When nosy outsiders came asking questions about the castle and its inhabitants, they were politely informed that the gentry minded their own business, and so did the townsfolk.

With a sigh the king sank into his favorite chair, the throne as the queen called it. "It's done, good people," he said to the assembled people sitting around the massive table. "We have our castle well protected and fully staffed, plus we've managed to bring the good folk of Kensington on side. Some we have compelled, most we have persuaded, and a few we have driven out. I believe we can call this one a win for now."

"Sire, this one will forever be a work in progress," said Amanda. "You know this."

"Yes, Amanda, I know, but I think we can relax our efforts there for the moment. Victor, how is our little project coming along?"

"It's ready, Sire. However, you know what this will mean if we have to use it."

"Yes, I do, but I see no other option."

"Harald, what are you two talking about?" asked Sally.

He gazed adoringly at her as he allowed his shoulders to slump. "Sally, my beloved, I'm unsure how to express this, but I must. You know full well, all of you, what Marlene has encountered on her journey. She seems to have become quite fond of the were-bear, but the snake man is another matter. This individual appears to be somewhat deranged."

"That and then some," sighed the queen. "He's every bit as crazy as Mobutu was. Have you devised a way to make an end of him permanently?"

"I believe I have, and I have a backup plan in the works. We can use the same method as we used with Mobutu, but we'll hold the ashes in a sealed container. If he manages to revive even after the fire, he will find himself in a small cell, deep within this castle, a cell with no door nor window, a cell from which there is no escape."

"Harald, that would mean he would slowly starve to death, over and over again for all eternity. Oh my husband, you can't do this, you can't."

"Nor do I wish to, my gentle love, but I need options and I see very few indeed for dealing with this creature."

She sighed and began to study her hands. "It's worse than you know."

"No, sweet Sally, Marlene checked in. I know what LeBlanc is doing. They were less than two weeks away, but this has driven them deep into the forest, and placed them in greater danger."

A tall exotic looking woman arose. "Do you want me to deal with this thing, Harald?"

"No, Ella, the trail and surrounding forest will be too full of hunters with weapons now. The tiger would be shot on sight. No, we must trust Marlene to get here on her own. Jimmy has delivered the antitoxin so she should be fine. She also has the aid of the were-bear. No, we must await the coming of the mad snake, and then deal with him."

"Harald ...?"

With a sigh the king gazed into the eyes of the queen and relented. "All right, my treasure, all right. Victor, can you modify the cell so we can feed the snake and keep it alive?" The other man nodded then arose to be about the task.

"People, if there are other options, I'd be willing to hear them."

"Well, Sire, there may be one alternative," said Clara Bynes.

"Clara?"

"This man is a snake, is he not? Does he therefore not need a warm climate? Would the cold not make him torpid? If he revives and has to occupy the cell forever, could we not keep the ambient temperature there somewhat colder? Keep him torpid? Better yet, place his ashes in a container of liquid nitrogen? Should that not prevent his revival?"

"Are you certain, Clara?"

"No, Sire, I'm just theorizing at this point."

"It does make sense," he agreed. "Can you prepare us a container? I know the cell sounds a bit barbaric, but, sadly, I have to confess, my thinking is still somewhat medieval at times." This brought a round of chuckles at his expense.

"All right, Clara, prepare us a more modern dungeon for our snake man. I believe my Sally will sleep more peacefully without that abomination running loose or alive and plotting in our basement."

THE FALLING RAIN WAS heavy with ice pellets, cold and chilling. LeBlanc huddled miserably under a fir tree, waiting out the storm. He was swearing to himself and praying the rain wouldn't wash away her trail when she moved. He wasn't even aware of the hawk perched in the upper branches of his tree.

He had successfully driven her off the path and into the deep woods, but the storm had come too quickly. Now all he could do was wait, watch, and wish he was beside that fire instead of them.

LILLY SAT AT HER COMPUTER, re-reading the one and only message she had received from Marlene. "Sweet Lilly, I haven't forgotten you. This is taking far longer than I'd hoped, and I am becoming tormented with us being so far apart. I swear I'll come for you the instant I'm free to do so. Don't forget me. Marlene."

It had come to her website and had gotten lost in the spam folder as her fan mail often did. It was only on one of her regular checks that she found it. Lilly had tried to send a reply, but wasn't able to bring herself to do so. Damn the vampire's compulsion anyway.

Marlene had left her the memories, but gave her a compulsion to keep them secret, also to not try to contact her until the mission was finished. So, until Marlene gave her the green light, Lilly was unable to even send her an e-mail acknowledging that she'd received the message.

She thumped her tiny fist on the desk then sighed and went to the window. It was raining hard, and she knew it would be a lot colder up on the trail, possibly even snow or freezing rain. "Gods, Marlene, I hope you found shelter before this hit. Be safe, my crazy woman."

Lilly watched the storm for a long time then returned to the desk. She took a sip of her now cold tea and returned to work. Reworking her vampire hero was taking more effort than she would have imagined. She had to be careful not to put too much of Marlene into the character.

Thinking of Marlene again, she allowed a wicked little grin to grace her lips. "What could it hurt if the hero was a heroine? Would her audience be scandalized if the girl in the book fell for a female vamp? Only one way to find out for sure. Lilly's fingers began to fly over the keyboard.

LILLY'S PRAYER FOR Marlene's safety had been answered. Not far from the snake man's hiding place, a cheery fire crackled in the mouth of a shallow cave. Marlene sighed with contentment and once again marveled at Torvil's survival skills. He'd spotted the cave, sensed the storm approaching, and suggested they hunker down until it blew itself out.

Keeping careful watch for LeBlanc, she helped him gather firewood then settled in. He lit the fire then began to cook the rabbit he'd killed.

"Torvil, can you see him?"

"Just barely. He might take a chance when darkness falls, but I doubt it. The cave mouth is too small; there's no way to sneak up on us. We could head out in the night, maybe ditch him then, let the rain wash away our trail."

"No, we want him to follow us. If it were just a matter of getting you home we would have taken Jimmy up on his offer of a ride."

"But the king wants this snake dead, so we lead him into the trap?"

"Damn straight."

Torvil chuckled. "Marlene, can I ask you something?"

"Shoot."

"You say you're over six centuries old, and lived all that time in Europe, yes?"

"Yep."

"All right, so how is it that, although you've only been in America for a couple of years, you speak like a native?"

She chuckled and gave him her brightest smile. "I practice," she replied. "Learning an accent is no different than learning a new language. The idea is to fit in, right? I practice constantly, and I will admit, there's something about drinking their blood that makes that a lot easier.

"So, what about you? I know you were a Russian nobleman for a few hundred years, yet you sound like a southern redneck. How does that happen?"

"Slowly over a hundred years or so of living and working with those folks. Can you tell me something else?"

"Sure."

"I've seen you hard and cold, but by nature you seem to be a bit more friendly. Is that a vampire thing, or ...?"

"Oh come on, you already know the answer to that one, Torvil. At first, when you realize what you are it scares the hell out of you, then you move to feeling superior to everyone else. Getting burned as a witch will knock that out of you in a hurry.

"I moved into self loathing for a few decades, tried the cold deadly assassin for a hundred years or so, outlived every friend and lover I ever knew, wallowed in heartbreak for a while, told myself they're just food for a time, hid in my mansion for a century or more, etc.

"You've been there, through it all, and probably more than I have. You also know that, especially for us, life goes on, and we might sulk for a decade or two, but sooner or later we have to crawl back out of the shell and move on."

"You're right, girl, I can't argue any of that, been through all of it too many times. So, does this mean you're going to go back for Lilly?"

"Yes I am, you savage old matchmaker you. Yes, I know what will happen. I'll enjoy a few years with her, but she'll start to age, then get afraid I'll leave her for someone younger, beg me to make her immortal, then eventually fall into acceptance as she realizes I'll never leave her, but will stay and love her as hard as I can for as long as I can.

"She'll never truly understand why I stay."

"Aging is a part of life," sighed Torvil. "A part we'll never experience, except through those we love."

"Yes. How many times have you grown tired of life, brother bear?"

"Far too many to count, you?"

"The same. I tried suicide once as well."

That made him laugh. "Didn't work, did it?"

"Nope, I just came back hungry and pissed off. Have you ever ...?"

"Oh yeah, a couple of times, usually after the death of a lover. Like you say, you just come back, hungry as hell, and mad at yourself for even trying. That's when you swear the oath, right?"

"The oath to suck as much joy out of life as possible while your lover is alive and then move on with grace?"

"Yeah, that one. You know, little sister, if Dorri had passed in her sleep, you and I would never have met."

"Yeah. Torvil, I'm really sorry for what happened to her, I am, but I'm glad we met."

"You sure weren't at first," he chuckled.

"No, I wasn't, I wanted to throttle you. Some days I still do. Just look at me for pity sake. This poor little princess hasn't had a bath in weeks, my clothes are in rags, my nails all jagged and broken, and I can only imagine what the hell my hair looks like. Thank the gods I don't have a mirror, or I'd likely fall into depression and kill myself."

She was smiling and he chuckled as he threw another branch on the fire. "So, what was the original plan?"

"Track you down and throw your sorry ass in the back of my car then take you straight to Harald and make him pay dearly for causing me miss my plane to Paris."

"Sorry to mess you up on that."

"The hell you are, Torvil the Bear. The hell you are. Hush, he's moving ... away, he's moving away, probably looking for better shelter. Dammit, I'm getting so sick of this."

"In a hurry to get back to a big-eyed girl?"

"Yes I am. Help me here, how do we make this happen?"

"I'm pretty well fed. You drink that last bottle before we head out, then we return to the trail and hot foot it to the castle."

"What about LeBlanc?"

"He's a hunter, so he'll be able to follow us if we leave him a reasonable trail, but we'll have to push hard enough so he can't get out in front and get up to mischief. The question is, are we close enough to get there before we have to feed again?"

"We are if we push hard. We'll be pretty worn down, but we can make it."

"Then we have a plan. Once the rain stops we head out and make a run for it, let the king's men deal with the snake."

"Torvil, you ever wonder if it's worth it all? You know, humanity? Have you ever just wanted to run away forever?"

"Too many times, little sister, too many times. I did too, at different points in my life. Gave it up and disappeared back into the forests, went bear, hibernated through the winters, wandered around enjoying the living forest all around me. A couple of times I stayed away from humans for decades or more. You?"

"Yeah, I've gotten sick of it and them all right, plenty of times."

"Have you ever just faded away for a few centuries?"

"Oh I've wanted to a few times, but I can't. I do need to feed, after all. Nuts and berries just won't do it for me." This brought a belly laugh from him and she smiled. "No, but sometimes I wonder about humans. They'll destroy everyone and everything in their path, and enjoy it, but if something kills or even frightens one of them then it has to die.

"They'd freak out and go on a killing spree to end all killing sprees if they found out about our existence. As long as vampires and were-bears are the stuff of scary stories to enjoy in complete safety they'll be fine, but if they find out we're real they'll hunt us to extinction.

"The thing is, they're destroying the entire world's ability to support life as we know it, but they don't seem to care, at least, not enough of them."

"That bothers you, doesn't it?"

"It sickens me, Torvil, but there doesn't appear to be much I can do about it at this point."

"I get that. So, can you tell me more about this sanctuary?"

"Brother bear, I have no idea what the king has in mind. I don't, but I can tell you this, Harald Eldredsson is our best bet for survival, especially in this political climate. He'll find a way to hide and protect his people.

"Mother once told me he was the most successful king his people had ever known. Unfortunately they discovered his true nature and drove him out. Within a generation they had been conquered twice and most of them carted off as slaves. That broke his heart and he went into hiding."

Torvil nodded. "So, what brought him back, to become the king again, I mean?"

"In a way, Mobutu did. You see, vampires are solitary hunters by nature, and somewhat territorial as well. Mobutu went on a killing spree, you know, killing the vampires so he could be the only one. He killed Gina and called the rest of us to gloat.

"That's when Harald and Gudrun called us all together. Mobutu could destroy us all one to one, so Harald convinced us to work together. When Mobutu captured Mother's lover and the woman who was to become Harald's queen, Mother, the strongest of us all, declared Harald the king. He accepted and so did we.

"Once he took charge as king, Mobutu soon found himself facing the saber-toothed tiger in battle with predictable results. Mobutu was killed, the body cremated, ashes scattered, and the rest is history.

"When it was over, Harald remained king by common consent. Later we discovered the werewolves, and they were eventually pulled into his domain. The king's driving motivation is to protect his people, and he understands that means keeping them out of the knowledge of humans.

"I expect that by sanctuary he means to find a way for you to survive and be yourself without drawing undo attention."

"That's pretty damned hard to do these days."

"Yes it is, but he has help. All the vampires, werewolves, and a dedicated team of human experts who have chosen to help us. These folks prefer to be governed by the king instead of the elected fools of the country.

"By the way Tommy's talking, I believe Harald's found a far more defensible location for our lair. He will surely have taken into account your predicament when he chose it."

"Why would he do that?"

"Because he's Harald Eldredsson, king of the non humans. He's accepted that role, he'll see himself as your king, and will do everything in his power to protect you."

"Yeah, what about that snake that's hunting us? Would he see himself as that man's king as well?"

"Yes, and he'll also see him as a traitor to his own kind. He'll probably execute him personally if we can't bring him down ourselves."

"We already did that. Didn't seem to work."

Marlene grinned. "I know. Harald will be working on it as we speak. By the time we get close, the king will be prepared, have no doubt of that."

Torvil was thoughtful for a while so she spoke again. "Don't even think of sneaking away and going full bear for a few centuries. You do and I'll track you down and drag your sorry butt back to..."

"Easy, my savage sister, easy," he grinned. "I promised I'd go with you and hear what your king has to say, and I will. I owe you that much and more. I'm just wondering about the possibilities, that's all. Get some rest now, I'll keep an eye on the snake."

The rain stopped in the night, but they waited until morning before setting out. They made their way carefully back to the Appalachian Trail, making sure soggy LeBlanc was following, then they set out at a run, Torvil in bear mode. Later that morning hikers saw a woman being chased by a bear. It looked like she was on the phone and a hawk was flying overhead.

TOMMY ANSWERED THE phone to hear heavy breathing. "Who are you and how did you get this number?"

"Tommy, it's Marlene."

"Miss Marlene? Are you all right?" He punched the button to put it on speaker. The king's head came up instantly.

"Fine, Tommy, I'm running. We're going slow enough so the snake can follow us, but fast enough to keep him out of trouble. Tell Harald to be ready for him, this bastard is treacherous and deadly."

"I hear you, Marlene," said Harald. "How close are you?"

"Three or four days at best guess."

"Can you make it without feeding?"

"That's the plan. See you soon." With that she broke the connection.

"Well, we're about out of time, people. Clara, is the prison ready?"

"It is, Sire. I have the nitrogen container in my lab, and Victor has prepared a special storage chest to place it in. All I need now are the ashes."

"I've made the arrangements with the crematorium, Sire," said Gudrun. "As soon as we bring them a body they'll dispose of it for us."

"And not remember they've done it?"

"Of course not."

"Well done, Gudrun, well done. So, now we wait. Does anyone know if her apartment is ready for her?"

"It's ready, Harald," said the queen, "and Gudrun has already stocked it with a few bottles of blood. Everything is waiting for her to arrive."

"All right then, now I should go practice with the sword if I'm going to kill a snake."

"Let me, great king."

"Illya?"

"The Children of the Wolf owe so much to you. Let us deal with the snake. We have the antivenin, do we not?"

"We do," said Tommy.

"Then let us deal with this creature."

Slowly, Harald nodded his head. "All right, llya, but be careful. This thing is faster than anything you've ever faced before. Perhaps you could herd it directly to me."

Illya nodded. "Perhaps you are wisest in this. The pack will bring it to you, King Harald." With that he rose and left the hall.

Three days of hard travel later, Marlene noticed the flicker out of the corner of her eye. She dropped to a walk then stopped and patted the bear. "Change back," she panted. Both she and Torvil looked haggard. Torvil shifted back to the man then quirked an eye at her. "What?"

"We can rest a bit now. They're here."

"Who?"

"Them," she replied as she pointed. He turned to see a pack of wolves appear out of the forest. Big wolves, wolves of a kind he hadn't seen for many centuries. Dire wolves. The alpha approached then shimmered into an older man. "It's good to see you, Illya."

"And you, Miss Marlene. Is the snake still behind you?"

"It is, you can catch its scent easily. Human and not human. Illya, be careful. This thing is fast and deadly."

"We have the antivenin," he replied, as he tapped the small pouch strapped around his neck. "We will be cautious. Our task is to make sure it finds its way to the king who awaits it with sword in hand."

"Now that's the best news we've had in a long time. Illya, how close are we?"

"You will be near the castle by nightfall. Nikka!" A young wolf trotted over to them. "Guide Miss Marlene to the castle then return to us."

She nudged him then set out at a gentle trot. Marlene and Torvil, now back in bear form, followed closely. "Dire wolves," thought Torvil. "Haven't seen any of those in the last few thousand years."

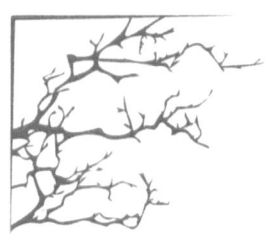

Home Coming

It was a beautiful morning, the sun just starting to show above the horizon and a hawk was lazily soaring overhead. Bill Walker sighed and smiled as he stepped from the house. This house wasn't the family farmhouse he'd been born in, and grew up in, but it was made to look as much like it as possible. They had also added lots of modern conveniences to make his life easier.

That being said, Bill was a farmer, by birth, by choice, and by nature. Smiling, he stuck his hands in his pockets and set out for the barn. He'd feed his few critters then do his patrol of the land. It was a perfect day for it, and he was happy to be alive.

The years had seemed to fall away as he slowly realized he didn't have to worry about making the bank payment, finding money for feed for the animals, nor did he have to wonder if he could manage to hire a few hands for the heavy work from time to time. All these things were being provided for him. Life was good.

He was whistling tunelessly as he entered the barn, then he stopped cold. There was a giant bear asleep on the barn floor and a small woman with red hair sleeping beside it on a pile of loose hay. With a grin of delight Bill took out the new phone young Tommy had showed him how to use.

"Harald here."

"Good morning, Sire," grinned Bill.

"What's on your mind, Bill?"

"Sir, I've got Goldilocks and Papa Bear asleep here in the barn. Thought you'd want to know."

162

"I'll be right there. Bill, better go in the house and start a bath running for her in case she's grouchy."

"I heard that," replied Bill, as he saw Marlene sit up and shake the hay from her hair.

She looked pretty haggard, but rose easily and stretched then poked the bear. "Up you get, lazy bones. If I'm up, you get up. Hi, Bill, long time, no see."

"It's good to see you alive, girl. You took your time getting here. King Harald said I should run you a bath. Should I?"

"I'll do it. You keep everybody out of the house until I come out, okay?"

"Do my level best."

"Awesome. Keep an eye on this grouchy old bear, would you?"

"Ah-huh. That Torvil?"

"It is."

"Tell him to change back to human form and I'll bring him some coveralls to pull on before the king gets here."

"Bit late for that," grinned Marlene, as the big car skidded to a halt in the barnyard. Sally was at the wheel.

Marlene picked more straw from her hair as Harald jumped out of the car and came to her. "You owe me, big time. You can start as soon as I get in the house and have a bath."

"Your apartment is waiting for you, and all your clothes are there. Go with Sally now and she'll take care of you." She nodded and started past him. "Marlene, I'm glad you're back and in one piece."

"I'm ready for that six weeks in Paris now. You promised."

"I did, and you've earned it. Do I get a hug before you go?"

"I stink like a goat and look like hell. You can hug me now, that's all you deserve." She stepped into his arms and hugged him.

"I was worried about you."

"Sure you were."

"I was, and you smell much better than you did after the Sweden adventure."

Marlene stepped back and scowled at him, but couldn't hold it, she broke into a wide smile and chuckled. "That's it for you, mister. I'm not talking to you anymore." She got in the car with Sally, and it sped away, back to the manor house.

Grinning, Harald turned back to the barn. The bear was watching him closely, its head tilted to one side, taking his measure. Neither of them moved for a moment and Bill slipped away to the house. Harald sighed and tossed aside his shirt then shimmered into full vampire mode. He flexed his powerful muscles and showed his claws.

"So, shall we do it this way like a couple of animals," he said, then shimmered back into the man and reached for his shirt, "or shall we behave like civilized men?"

The bear reared up to its twelve feet of height then shimmered into a short, powerfully built man with heavy coarse features. He stepped forward then dropped to one knee. "Greetings, King Harald. Torvil Reyburne at your service."

"That's right pretty, Torvil," said Bill, as he returned with clothes for him, "but it'd be more impressive with pants on. Here, get dressed. You're scaring the chickens."

Torvil laughed so hard he actually fell over. Bill tossed him the clothes and he pulled them on. "Better?"

"Much," said Harald, as he offered his hand and pulled the other man to his feet. "So, you've been in a royal court before."

"It's been a while. But yes, I have. Forgive me, Sire. We didn't have a lot of leisure on the road for etiquette lessons. I'll need some guidance if you decide to keep me alive."

"My court is quite informal, Torvil. Keep you alive? Didn't Marlene tell you we're offering sanctuary?"

"She mentioned something about that, but I expected you'd want to make that judgment for yourself."

"Marlene already made that decision, my friend, otherwise you wouldn't be here." Just then the big car returned. "Come on, you look half-starved and exhausted. We'll get you fed and give you a place to rest. Take a few days to get back on your feet then we'll talk about what we can do for each other."

"Each other? As I recall monarchy rules, it's about what use you can be to the king. As you can see I'm a bit of a standout in public. What could I possibly do for you that would give you a reason to keep me alive?"

Harald sighed and allowed his shoulders to relax. "There are dozens of possibilities, Torvil, and we'll discuss them after you've had a chance to recover. Right now we're still getting organized in our new home here, so I'll attend to that while you rest up. Please understand, I have no reason at all to harm you, and plenty of reasons to keep you alive."

Two days later Torvil, dressed like a gentleman from the late Victorian Era, was led by a servant to the great hall where Harald was conferring with several others. "Ah, Torvil, I see they found you some decent clothes."

Grinning his delight, he replied. "Indeed, my king. I feel quite my old self. I can't thank you enough for this."

"Excellent. It was a stroke of pure luck for us to find a costumer to make you some clothes. Now, we have much to discuss, my friend. Come with me."

The king led Torvil into what would become the library. The room was huge and filled with bookshelves, some filled, others not. There were two reading nooks with plenty of natural light and comfortable chairs. A set of stairs led to a wide mezzanine which also had a reading nook as well as bookshelves lining the walls.

"This is, or will be when it's finished, the library. The books you see were already here and my collection is in those boxes."

"I envy you this, King Harald, I do. When it's done it'll be nearly as big as the one I had in Russia a century or more ago."

"Oh? You said *had*. Did something happen to it?"

"Yes. The Bolsheviks came through and burned it to the ground. I fled west. I miss that library, used to spend weeks at a time in there. I collected old volumes and would often open one up just to admire the script."

"You sound wistful as you speak of it," smiled the king. He eased himself into a chair and indicated Torvil should sit.

"Yes, I guess I am wistful. If you decide to let me live is there any chance I might spend a few hours in here?"

"If death was to be your fate, Torvil my friend, you would never have seen this castle. I will admit I've been puzzled as to what we could do for you, but now I have the answer."

"You do?"

"Torvil, I'd like you to take over as the official librarian. You'd have to spend much of your time in here, but the wolves can show you the hidden pathways when you get the urge for a run through the trees."

Torvil's lips moved, but no sound came out. Finally he swallowed hard then spoke. "Are you serious?"

"Utterly. I need somebody to do this, and I don't have the time to do it myself. I warn you, I'll probably be in here taking up space quite often, for my library has often been my refuge in the past.

"I also think your idea of collecting old volumes is a good one. I was an antiques dealer back in London. I still have a few connections, perhaps we could work on that together."

"I'm a bit overwhelmed here," replied Torvil. "I don't know what to say."

"You could start by saying yes," grinned Harald.

"Yes, oh yes indeed. Harald, why? Why bother with me at all? It would be a lot simpler to just kill me, safer for you too."

"Now where would be the fun in that? Besides, have you any idea how hard it is to find a librarian with first hand knowledge of older volumes?" Harald grinned as he rose to his feet. "Stay here and familiarize yourself with the layout, get a few ideas of how you want to go about this.

"I'll send Tommy to you after a while, and he can help locate anything you might need." He patted his new friend on the shoulder and walked away.

A while later Torvil was standing at the window gazing out over the tennis courts towards the trees, a book in his hand.

Footsteps from behind alerted him to company and he turned to see Marlene smiling at him. She looked so different, like a young debutante. "So, the king tells me you're the new librarian."

"Marlene, I can't begin to tell you what a gift this is to me. I know I dare not go out in public again, but I can be happy here for centuries. I have the books, the forest close by, and a friend who wants to help me re-establish my favorite hobby."

"You won't miss being out among people?"

"No, why would I? There are people here, intelligent, interesting, people, the vampires, werewolves, the human allies,... gods girl, what more could this old caveman want?"

"Pretty girls?"

"Oh no, they're my weakness, they always get me in trouble."

Marlene laughed with delight then hugged him. "I'm happy for you, Torvil. Truly, I am. I'm off to find Lilly, and then to Paris for a mad shopping and pampering spree. I'll tell you all about it when I get back."

As she walked away another woman entered. This woman had a careworn face and seemed to be all business, but Torvil sensed there was more to her. He'd met her briefly when they'd arrived.

"Amanda, right?" he asked, as she approached.

"Yes, and you are Torvil. You're to be in care of the royal library, are you not?"

"Yes, I guess I am," he said with a smile. "How can I be of service to such a beautiful and charming woman?"

His flattery stopped her and caused her to blush. It was something Amanda was unaccustomed to. She recovered quickly, however, smiling in response to the merriment in his eyes.

"I've come to tell you a secret, good sir. This was once my grandfather's library. Grandfather was/is a complete paranoid, and so he had a secret built into this room. A secret a man of your obvious intelligence and unique nature might enjoy."

"Oh, oh, you've been talking to Marlene, and she's told you of my weakness for beautiful women, and my deep need for having my ego stroked. I warn you, Amanda, keep this flattery up and I'll be putty in your hands forever."

She laughed with delight and blushed slightly. "I warn you, sir, I will abuse that bit of information every chance I get. Now, come with me and I'll show you a secret."

He offered his arm and she took it, leading him to one of the reading nooks. "This was Grandfather's favorite reading chair. He loved the solitude here, but also wanted a bolt hole close at hand in case of emergency."

She stepped to the closest bookcase. "See these two volumes of War and Peace? The second is for reading. This first one has another purpose. Observe."

She pulled back on the book and there was an audible click. The bookcase moved slightly away from the wall. "It's rather well balanced with a pulley system," she said as she easily moved the heavy looking case aside, exposing a small room behind it.

"I wonder if they have the power to this... yes." She flicked on a light and stepped into the room, gently pulling Torvil along with her. She turned and took the handle, pulling the bookcase back into place with an audible click.

"This panel slides aside so you can peek in to be certain no one sees you return. This catch releases the bookcase to open the door."

She turned him and showed him the stairs leading down. "That passage will lead you into the tunnels and out into the forest unseen." She turned back and opened the door to the library again.

"I thought a man of your discerning nature, and love of the forest, would find a use for this little secret," she said, as they stepped through and she closed the door again.

"Brains, beauty, and she brings me gifts of untold value. I'm utterly besotted, Lady Amanda."

"You sir, are a complete master of the art of flattery. Marlene neglected to tell me this," smiled Amanda.

"She doesn't know," he grinned in reply. "She's quite pretty as a girl, but her vampire scares the bejeebers out of me."

Amanda laughed at that, and he grinned with delight. "That's the second time you've made me laugh, Torvil Reyburne. Be warned, I'll visit this library often, and I'll expect a full ration of that magic charm each time I do."

"I'll practice while I'm waiting for your return, dear lady."

Amanda patted his arm as she walked away. "Somehow I doubt that you need to practice."

He watched her go then sighed, sank back into a chair, and picked up the book he'd chosen to read, an old favorite. "Yes indeed, I do believe I'm going to like it here."

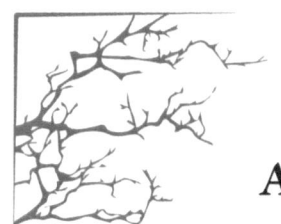

Alone no Longer

Once again Lilly stood gazing out the window and a light drizzle falling. She sighed, for it had been yet another week without a word from Marlene. She was worrying herself into a state of depression while, far away, Marlene sank into a sea of bubbles for the first time in months.

While Lilly gave in to the tears, Marlene groaned with delight and drained the second bottle of blood Gudrun had left for her. She set aside the bottle then sighed. Lilly's despair was trying to settle in on her heart. "Soon, my love, soon. Be patient with me for just another day or two."

The king was dressed in heavy leather armor, carrying his broadsword and long dagger as Marlene found him heading the tunnel to the forest. "Harald."

"Marlene, off to Paris?"

"Yes, but first I need to ask ..."

"Sally says to bring her here. It seems our Queen is a fan of Lilly Reilly, the author. That is the name of the woman you met on the trail, isn't it?"

"Oh don't look so smug. I have to talk to the queen about spoiling all my fun. Harald, is it truly all right if I bring her here?"

"We've all brought our lovers here, Marlene. Bring her here so we can help keep her safe for you."

"Harald, you're the best," she said, as she hugged him for a moment. "I see you have your armor on. Off to kill a snake?"

"Indeed I am."

"Be careful, Harald. This thing is terribly fast and cunning."

"I will. Ring me from Paris and I'll give you a blow by blow. Go on now, your lover is waiting." She kissed his cheek then hurried away to where Eric was waiting with the car. She would catch a ride to the city with Eric and Gudrun who would drop them off at the airport.

LILLY SAT AT HER COMPUTER writing furiously, the words pouring from her fingertips and onto the page. Soft romantic music was playing in the background as, with a pencil clenched tightly between her teeth, she labored on.

It had been over a month since her encounter with the vampire. She had given up all hope of seeing the object of her desire again, but at least she had the stories to write. Oh she'd changed them, changed them completely, but they were there.

Just as she'd promised she'd allowed the stories Marlene and Torvil had told her to stimulate her imagination, but she didn't actually use the tales they told in any recognizable form.

Dammit, maybe she should have. Maybe then Marlene would have to come back to kill her. At least that way she'd get to see her again, at least for a moment before she died. With a sigh Lilly stopped writing and walked to the window to stare out. She couldn't get Marlene out of her mind.

Tears began to flow freely down her cheeks as she gazed out at streets shiny and slick from the rain. The rain was depressing and that suited her mood perfectly. "Dear gods I'm a hot mess," she sniffed aloud.

"God, Marlene, how I wish you could have loved me the way I love you. I wish you had drained me and left my body in the woods rather than leave me like this. I know I should forget this foolish crush and move on, but I just can't seem to get you out of my mind."

Suddenly Lilly froze, a soft feminine voice was reading aloud the last passage she'd written.

"The woman gazed out over the cliff toward the heaving ocean. Tears of heartbreaking loss and despair flowed down her cheeks, mixing with the rain and salt spray that lingered there. She was gone. The vampire who'd courted her until Maggie surrendered her soul to her had vanished in the night. She'd taken her blood and her heart with her. Closing her eyes to the world that rejected her, she slowly toppled over the edge. 'Goody bye, my love,' she breathed as she fell.'

"Not bad. Not too bad at all, but a bit mellow dramatic, wouldn't you say?"

Lilly just stared open mouthed at the beautiful, impeccably dressed, woman who stood smiling at her. "So, did you miss me?"

"Marlene," she cried as she threw herself into the woman's arms. "Oh gods, Marlene, I gave up hope you'd come. I thought you'd forgotten all about me."

Marlene held the trembling, sobbing woman gently. "How could I possibly forget the woman who nearly drove me mad with her endless questions, and those big puppy dog eyes."

"Oh Marlene..."

"Hush now, sweet Lilly. You've felt the vampire's bite, now taste her kiss." She brought her lips to Lilly's and held her tightly.

Lilly moaned under the fire of that kiss. She felt as though her bones were melting and her body melding into the woman who held her so tightly. "Oh gods, do that again," she sighed as their lips slowly parted.

"I will, my sweet girl, I'll do that a hundred times a day for a century or two if you want me to."

Lilly's eyes were closed and a dreamy smile graced her lips. "Oh yeah, I do want you to do that, every day for a century, you promised."

"Yes I did," smiled Marlene, nuzzling at her neck and eliciting a soft intake of breath. "Now, you go start packing."

"Packing? Where am I going?" asked Lilly, as warm sweet breaths across the nape of her neck sent shivers of delight up her spine.

"I'm carrying you off to Paris for a month, and then I'm whisking you away to live with me in a castle, where you can write to your heart's content. You'll be surrounded by vampires, were-wolves, were-bears, European mercenaries, former CIA agents, enthralled servants, and god knows what else. Think you can deal with all that?"

"If you promise to kiss me like that every day, hell yes."

"Then get packing, my darling girl. We have a plane to catch."

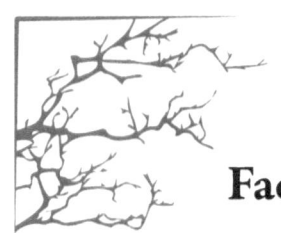

Facing a Hard Truth

While Marlene soaked away the weeks of forest running, dreaming of the day she would whisk Lilly away to a grand hotel suite in Paris, the hunter huddled in the cold beneath the trees. He'd tracked her to a small farm, but realized she was gone when he tried to get close. There were many scents there, the woman, the bear, but wolves who were not wolves and more blood drinkers as well.

"This is all wrong, Cher. Wrong. Too many to hunt. Too many to kill. Cold, Cher. Much too cold. Hard to think, Cher, hard to think. LeBlanc should go home, yes? Home to the warm lands, the warm swamps. LeBlanc don' like this cold place, Cher. We go home now, come back next summer. We claim the blood drinker then, Cher. Claim her then." With that he turned his steps south.

However, it wasn't going to be that easy. It was far too late for LeBlanc to abandon the hunt now.

The phone was answered on the first ring. "Tommy."

"Mr. Tommy, is King Harald there?"

"Right here, Illya. What's happened?"

"The snake man travels south, Sire. I don't think he likes the cold. We followed his scent and found where he'd been. He circled the farm, but didn't approach. Now he goes south."

"Stop him, Illya, head him off."

"We go, Great King." The connection was broken and the king began to pace.

"Illya's probably right," said Gudrun. "He's a warm climate snake, won't like the cold. Marlene's reached safety and he must know he'll never be able to get to her."

174

"I wouldn't go that far," said Amanda. "Yes, he may be retreating to a warmer clime, but he is utterly fixated on killing and eating her to gain her power."

"Moron," muttered Gudrun.

"Go on, Amanda," said the king.

"If we let him go he'll most likely return when the seasons warm," she said.

"Even without that, we need to get him out of circulation. He's drawn a lot of unwanted attention to that Appalachian trail. I want that thing out of the public eye. Opinions?"

"We're all agreed, Harald," replied Gudrun. "Do you want us to deal with him?"

"No, the wolves will herd him back to where I can make an end of him. I want you and your people to sweep a large area around that trail, make sure there is no curiosity aimed at our direction. Terry, you and your team make certain there is no government interest."

"Consider it done, Sire," replied Terry. They all left the great hall and the king headed for his exercise room. The queen found him there strapping on his armor.

"Harald?"

"Yes, my love, I go to deal with the snake. My old leather armor will stop the snake's fangs easier than Clara's spandex suit. I won't need to change to killing mode for this, I just need my sword."

"Harald, please be careful."

"I will, sweet Sally. We have the antivenin just in case. I'll deal with this then be home in time for the evening feast."

"The evening feast?"

He grinned wickedly as he pulled her tightly to him. "Yes, the evening feast, you know what I'm like after a battle."

"Harald, behave yourself. What if the servants were watching?" She was blushing and he smiled his delight. "Go on, you lascivious beast, go make an end of that monster then hurry back to me." She kissed his cheek then danced away from him, and blew him a kiss.

He waved and headed for the tunnel to the forest behind the castle. The hawk was circling high above the trail.

Out in the forest, things for LeBlanc were getting tense. He went from slinking away to running as fast as he could. Once he reached the trail he picked up the pace, but they were there, he could sense them. Wolves, but not wolves.

As he began to tire he sensed his doom. The alpha was pacing him, just out of reach. He lunged at the beast, but somehow it had read his intent and dodged aside, taking a bite out of his arm in the process.

Enraged, he attacked, but didn't reach the alpha. Two others took him from behind. As fast as he was, he was still grabbed by the hamstring and whipped into the air. He whirled around to attack this new adversary, but the alpha got his leg and jerked him away. His attempt to bite the wolf missed.

LeBlanc fled back into the trees and the wolves seemed to be content to let him go, but they stayed behind him, around him, always near, but just beyond reach. Darkness fell and they did not relent. He made several attacks, but they always thwarted him. No matter which wolf he lunged at, there were always more behind him, biting him, dragging him back.

Again and again he escaped only to find them still near, pacing behind and beside him, just out of reach in the forest. Slowly the reality of his situation began to seep into his deranged mind. They weren't trying to kill him, they were driving him before them, forcing him to return toward the blood drinker.

"So, dis be the way of it, Cher. De wolves push LeBlanc back to the blood drinker. Slow down now, Cher. The fight is not with brother wolf, Cher. It be with the drinker of blood. Is that it, Mr. Wolf? Do you take LeBlanc back to the woman who drinks blood?"

Even as he asked the question he saw the alpha in the moonlight. It shimmered into an old man and pointed back towards the farm where the blood drinker had disappeared. Before he could move to attack, the man became the wolf again and vanished into the gloom of night.

The sun was rising, trying to burn off the mist that had arisen during the cold of darkness. A rock face stopped LeBlanc's progress and he turned at bay, the wolf pack facing him, the hawk watching from high above. Slowly, out of the mist, walked a big powerfully built man wearing leather armor and carrying a long sword easily in his hand.

LeBlanc raised his head and sniffed the air. "Ah, another blood drinker. The woman's mate perhaps, Cher. So, you come to fight LeBlanc? To defend your woman, yes?"

"Not to fight you, snake," rumbled that deep voice as the man easily swept the gleaming sword through the air. "I've come to kill you and make sure you stay that way."

"Ah, then, Cher. Come to LeBlanc."

As Harald took a step forward the snake struck. The creature's speed was amazing, and it was well inside the reach of the deadly sword, it's fangs reaching for his neck, when its life ended. Blood spattered everywhere and the snake man's body slammed into the king, causing him to take a step back, but it was dead.

The sword had been a decoy. Harald knew of the creature's speed and so he baited it with the sword. As the snake sped past the long blade, the dagger, sped by a mighty arm, reached its neck, severing the head from the shoulders. The body lay twitching at his feet, and he kicked it away.

Two men in military uniform stepped from the trees and stuffed the body into a body bag while a tall golden-haired woman scooped the head into a sack and followed them away.

The king nodded approvingly as he watched them go, then slung his sword over his broad shoulder and headed back toward the tunnel to the castle, the wolf pack trotting along behind him.

The Hawk Revealed

Bill Walker had finished his morning stroll around the perimeter of the two farms. He grinned to himself as he watched Olla trot back to the castle in wolf form. Once she'd disappeared through the gate he glanced at the sky. The hawk still soared high above.

"Every instinct I've got tells me you're one of them. Are you planning to come down here and talk to me or not?" The bird just lay on the air currents, gazing down at him. "All right, tell you what. You folk always come up buck naked when you shift back to human. I know that not everybody's as comfortable that way as Olla and Torvil, so I'll leave the upper door of the barn open, and I'll hang a robe on a nail for you. You know, just in case you decide you want to talk.

"I'll just go for that robe now." He grinned as he turned away. Bill was fully aware as the bird swept down to perch on a nearby tree to keep an eye on him. He disappeared into the house for a moment then returned carrying a white bathrobe. He carried it to the barn then hung it on a peg just inside the door. He turned back and walked out of the barn.

Bill was startled as the hawk swept from the tree and past his head, nearly knocking his hat off. He spun around to see the bird morph into a naked woman just as it alit. Her bare feet touched the floor and in a single stride she had the robe about her shoulders, and was tying the belt loosely about her waist.

Doing his best to remain calm, he watched her step towards him. Swallowing hard, Bill found his voice. "Mornin', miss. Name's Bill Walker. Is there anything I can get for you?"

178

Amber eyes that were slowly turning blue watched him closely. She seemed to shake herself then spoke hesitantly, as though she wasn't accustomed to human speech anymore. "I'd kill for a cup of coffee."

"Right this way, ma'am. I'll put on a fresh pot." He led her into the farmhouse kitchen then dutifully began to build up a pot of coffee. "You like it strong?"

"Not too strong, please, Mr. Walker."

"Bill, call me Bill. Medium brew is my favorite too." He started the machine then brought mugs, cream, and sugar to the table. He sat across the table from her and smiled. "Thanks for dropping in. I was starting to worry you might be a government agent or something."

That brought a smile to her face. "I was once," replied the athletic looking woman, "in a manner of speaking. I was a wildlife officer up until a few weeks ago."

"Oh? What happened? Quit the job?"

"No, you know damn well what happened."

"Actually, I know what you are, but, not how you managed to get there, or when it happened."

"Really, so just what am I, Mr. Bill Walker?"

"I imagine the answer to that would be a were-hawk. You know, a human who can change into an animal. Actually we call them non-humans."

"So, you believe I can change back into the hawk again? Back and forth at will?"

"Convinced of it. I take it this is something new for you."

"Yes. I was trying to free a hawk from a power line when someone turned the power back on. I felt the jolt of electricity, and the hawk sank its beak into my neck at the same time. We fell onto a rock that exploded into a green mist and I passed out from the pain. The next thing I knew I was looking down at the world.

"It took a number of days for me to clear my mind of the hawk's natural drives."

"Is that when you spotted the little gal and the bear?"

"Yes, and that snake thing that was hunting them. That thing was evil, pure evil. The hawk knew. I tried to warn them, but they didn't understand."

"You kept an eye on them anyway."

"Yes, I wanted to help them, but didn't know how. Yesterday I saw that big man kill the snake. You have to warn them, it will revive."

"They already know, and are well prepared for that. They'll deal with the snake, don't worry."

"What are they?"

"Non-humans."

"The wolf that walks with you, she's one of them, isn't she?"

Bill smiled at that. "Yes, Olla's one of them. I first met her as a woman. I made the mistake of saying I wanted a dog to walk with me in the mornings. Next morning she showed up, changed into the wolf, then followed me around the farm. She's done it every day since. It scared the bejeebers out of me the first time. Her husband says she does it so he'll have to make breakfast for the kids."

Again she smiled. "What more can you tell me about what I've become, Mr. Walker?"

"Bill, please, Ma'am. Call me Bill."

"Sorry, Bill. I'm Rhonda Stockman, Dr. Rhonda Stockman. I'm a veterinarian, or at least I was. Please call me Ronnie, everybody does, I mean did."

"Actually, Ronnie, the folks in the castle could be a lot more help to you than I can. I'm just the gate watcher, you know, keeping an eye out for odds and ends, as well as providing a bit of fresh food for the castle."

She looked dubious, frightened, so he went on. "Ronni, you can trust those folks. Yes, the king killed the snake, but he did it to protect the little gal and the bear."

"The were-bear." He nodded and poured her another coffee. "I confess I do need help, and I have no idea where to turn for it. I know damn well if I go to the authorities I'll be locked up and studied, turned into a weapon, or worse. Dissected maybe. Are you sure I can trust these people?"

"I sure would."

"I saw that girl change many times and she attacked people. Is she a ...?"

"Vampire?"

She swallowed hard and her voice shook as she replied. "Yes."

"Yeah, she is. So's the king and several others. No, I'm not one of them. Yes, I do trust them. Ronnie, they'll never hurt a friend, and they don't kill unless there's no other way. You really should talk to them."

She sighed deeply and fairly melted into the chair. "Are you sure they'll help me?"

"Absolutely."

"All right, how do I contact them?"

"I can do it for you, if you'd like."

She nodded so he took out his phone and called. "Harald here. What's up, Bill?"

"Lady Hawk is here in the kitchen drinking all my coffee," he grinned. "Sire, the lady is all brand new to the changing thing, and she's a bit spooked. Perhaps Queen Sally might come to talk to her."

"On my way," sang a woman's voice.

Bill smiled and set aside his phone. "Sally is queen of these folks. She's not a vampire or a shape-shifter, but she's scary psychic and a real sweetheart. You'll like her."

"She's human?"

"Yes."

"That's why you asked for her." He nodded. "Thanks for that."

He smiled and refilled her mug. It was only moments before the car arrived in the driveway. A soft knock at the door then she entered. Ronnie had no idea what she was expecting, but whatever it was, this wasn't it. The woman was quite pretty, but dressed in a tee shirt and jeans, not an expensive gown. "Coffee, Sally?"

"I'll get it, Bill. Thanks."

"Ronnie, this is Queen Sally. Ma'am, this is Dr. Rhonda Stockman, also known as the hawk. Now, I've got chores to do, so I'll leave you folks to it."

As Bill walked out the door Sally passed a bag to Ronnie. "Try these on, see if they fit."

Ronnie looked in the bag and saw a pair of sweats, sports bra and panties, and a pair of flip flops. She quickly shed the robe and dressed herself while the queen poured and fixed her coffee.

Sally smiled as she turned back and sat facing the nervous woman. "So, you're the mystery hawk who's been following our Marlene all summer."

"Yes, I guess I am. You're the vampire queen. Am I supposed to kneel, or..."

"Whoa, easy girl. Sally will do just fine. The older folk among us who're more accustomed to royal courts and such call me Majesty, Queen Sally, or Ma'am. The Americans call me Sally. You sound like an American to me, so Sally will be fine. Ronnie is it?"

The woman nodded, somewhat overawed by the queen. Sally had changed a lot in the years she'd been married to Harald. She now wore an air of authority as easily as most people wear a favorite tee shirt. "Okay, Ronni, Bill says you're new to the change. Can you talk about that?"

"Yes. Bill says he trusts you people. He said you'd help me."

"We will, I promise. Tell me about the change now."

"Yes, well, I have no idea how it happened, but it did. It took me days to clear my mind and think straight again. It took even longer to feel at ease in the air, and I still don't like killing for food, but I have to eat. Right, the change.

"Well, once I understood what had happened, and what I'd become, I didn't know what to do. I was a bird, and I couldn't change back. In my mind I was still me, but I couldn't change back.

"I was resigned to my fate when I spotted the girl and the bear. The bear changed into a man and back to a bear. From that moment on I followed them, trying to believe if he could do it then maybe I could learn how to change back too.

"I saw that snake man hunting them and tried to warn them, but I failed in that. Anyway, to make a long story short, I followed them to this farm. The farmer seemed like such a kind man, much like my grandfather, so I stayed around. Suddenly I realized he was actually talking to me, wanting me to change back and talk to him.

"He brought a bath robe out to the barn for me and that did it. I needed to change back so badly I suddenly felt it start to happen. He brought me inside, calmed me down, gave me coffee, then called you. Bill said you'd help me. Will you? Can you?"

"We'll do everything we can, I promise, Ronnie. We'll set you up with rooms, top floor with a high view I think. I'm sorry, Ronnie, you won't be able to go back to your old life again, but you're welcome at the lair."

"The lair?"

"The mansion. Harald calls it the castle, but I call it the Vampire's Lair. We have many people living there, both human and non-human. We'll help you gain a greater understanding of what you've become, and how to take joy in that. We'll also do whatever we can to help you gain mastery over the change. Perhaps Torvil would be the best bet for that, Torvil or Ella."

Sally saw the bewildered look on Ronnie's face. She smiled and patted the woman's hand. "The vampires don't fully change into the original beast, except one. Ella changes into the saber-toothed tiger. Torvil is the bear you're already familiar with. Those two fully change, so they're the most likely to help you master it."

"All right, I guess..."

"You're frightened, and overwhelmed, I know. Would you rather stay here at the farm for a few days until you have time to mull it over?"

"Yes, no, I don't know." Her hands were trembling, and she was close to tears. Ronnie gave a small gasp of shock as Sally reached for and took her hands. The warmth and gentle calm seemed to flow from the queen to her and she shuddered then relaxed. Sally gave her hands another gentle squeeze then released her.

"Thank you for that, Sally. You're right, I'm terrified and I don't understand any of this. Please help me. I'll do whatever you say."

"Then I say you need a few days of rest and relaxation. One of our people is a psychiatrist. I'll ask Amanda to help you sort through it. Would that be acceptable to you?" Ronnie nodded and Sally reached for her phone.

"Elaine here, how may I serve?"

"Elaine, it's Sally. We're having a guest for a few days. Make up a room on the top floor, one with a view, please."

"At once, Ma'am."

"Also, Dr. Stockman will need clothes, so see what you can do for her once she arrives. Oh, and ask Amanda to meet us when we arrive if she's free."

"Yes, my Queen, I'm on it. Perhaps a few snacks in the room as well?"

Sally laughed with delight. "Just do your thing, Elaine. I have every faith you'll make it perfect."

She closed the connection and returned the phone to her shoulder bag. "That girl is a wonder. We'll just finish our coffee then return to the Lair.

"Ronnie, thank you for trusting us, and believe me, I'm thrilled that you came to us for help. We'll get you through this, help you come to terms with who and what you've become."

"And then decide if I need to be killed or not?"

"That's not on the table, girl. There's a reason Bill called for me and not someone else."

"He said you're the queen."

"I am. I'm also psychic. If I'd sensed any danger to my people from you I'd have called Harald with a coded message. I sense no danger from you at all, but my maternal instincts are going crazy. I just want to hug you and tell you it will all be fine."

"Oh god, I'd like that ..." suddenly the woman burst into tears. She was in Sally's arms instantly, being gently rocked and soothed. "Sorry. I didn't mean to do that," she sniffed.

Sally gave her another motherly squeeze then kissed the top of her head and released her. "I know, but you've been through a lot recently. It's all right to lean on a friend. Come on. Let's get you home." She took Ronnie by the hand and led her out to the car.

She sat in the big car, watching as the farm gave way to the castle grounds. She'd been afraid that those walls would be a prison, but once inside the grounds she suddenly felt protected. Somehow, this change that had terrified her, then filled her with a pit of despair, had brought her the one thing she'd always dreamed of having. A place she could call home, where she could feel safe from a savage world.

Later that night, as she crawled into the luxurious bed, she marveled at how her life had changed again. No more lonely basement apartment, no more huddling in trees from the rain, but safe and warm in a new home. She'd bathed, eaten, then been introduced around, spent time talking with Amanda, and then returned to her room to read.

"I'm going to like living here in the Lair," she smiled to herself as she turned out the light.

"WELL, MY KING?" ASKED Gudrun.

"I'm well pleased, Gudrun. We have our stronghold, we have it well protected, we've eliminated the threat of the snake man, pulled in the were-bear and the hawk-woman. All in all, I think I can take a day or two to see how Torvil is making out in the library. For the moment, all seems to be under control."

"You won't mind if we paranoids keep an eye out for trouble, do you?"

"Not at all," he chuckled, as he rose to his feet. Taking his queen by the hand, he left for the royal chambers.

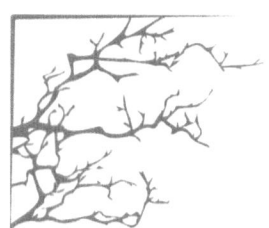

The End

Author's note: So, ready for a peek at the next installment? It's a tale of hawks, werewolves, vampires, and so much more. It begins in a secret government lab...

The Hawk and Wolf

by

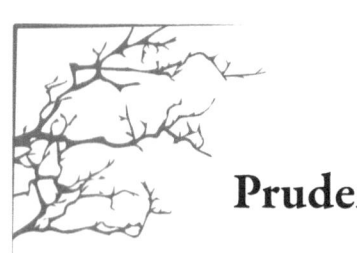

Prudence MacLeod

Mystery and Mayhem

The door to the lab swung open and another student rushed in. "You're late," said a voice that he ignored. "Bring me that box over there, help me get it open."

"It's heavy ..."

"Don't drop it." There was a sudden explosion as the box hit the floor, and a green dust settled over everyone and everything amid the screams of the injured.

TWO MEN STOOD SILENTLY gazing at the mayhem and destruction that lay before them, separated from it only by a thin sheet of glass. This had been a government lab, a room where people in lab coats poked at this and that, and then wrote notes on clip boards. What could have happened to cause this?

The place was shattered, everything broken and thrown around as though a cyclone had gone through the room. Also, bits and pieces of human and animal flesh were scattered around, and that's what had them both fighting to keep from losing their last meal.

They could see clearly that several pieces of the dead were a mix of animal and human remains, fused together as though some mad god had tried to make new creatures by meshing them together, but failed. Many had obviously been torn apart.

"Sir?"

"Jesus, Egan, what the hell happened here?"

190

"We don't know, sir, but we've sealed off the building. Only a handful of people have seen this and two are dead already."

"Excuse me?"

"That green dust all over everything, sir. Apparently, it's highly toxic. Director Compton, what do you want to do here?"

The tall, thin, man sighed deeply then turned away from the glass that separated them from the destroyed lab. A tight feeling in his gut told him the choices here would be bad and worse. A slight pain in his chest was ignored as he replied to his companion.

"I want this explained in a way I can convince the senate committee that's it's all a natural occurrence. Hell, I want someone to convince me it's a natural occurrence, not an attack by some foreign power, aliens from space, or demons from hell. Once I have that, I want it all to go away.

"Put the special team on it immediately."

"I tried, sir. Two agents refused to touch it and three others quit. The psychic checked himself into a locked ward. Sir, that green dust, it does something to the mind as well as the body."

"Dammit, we've got to keep a lid on this. We can't let the media or the public get wind of it. All right, I'm wide open to suggestions here."

"Sir, you know what you have to do. There's only one man who ..."

"Oh no, there's no way in hell I'm letting him or any of those people ..."

"Sir, I honestly can't see another option, unless you want to call in the military ..."

"No, no military, no EPA, no disease control ... Ah, shit, as badly as I hate to admit it, you're right. There's only one man capable of dealing with this and keeping it under the radar. I'll make the call."

They walked outside and locked the building behind them. With sagging shoulders, he leaned against the car and pulled out his phone. A moment later he sighed deeply and tossed the phone onto the seat of the car.

"Nothing. The bastard has changed his phone to an unlisted number. All right, keep a lid on this and track him down for me."

"Yes, sir. Sir, what do you think will happen if we can't find him?"

"Then we're screwed. Come on, he's a private eye, P.I.s need work, he can't be that damned hard to find."

AS THE TWO MEN CLIMBED back into the car and drove off, a thin, stooped, woman hurried away, clutching the scarf around her face tightly. She crawled into her own car and, struggling with her misshapen clawed hands, managed to get the key into the ignition and start the engine. She'd heard every word the men had spoken, and although she had no idea who would be coming after her, she didn't want to be found. Not like this.

She drove slowly, carefully, out of the city and into the hill country beyond. She had to find a place to hide. She'd give it a few days, then return to the site of the first accident. Perhaps she'd find an answer there, she had to find an answer.

A few days later, she reached the original sight, the place where it had all begun. It had been cleaned up and there was nothing there except dust and dirt, a discarded cigarette pack and a beer can. A woman she'd worked with had disappeared from this spot months before, only her clothes were left behind. It was ruled a kidnapping by slavers, but she didn't believe it, not now. There'd been hawk feathers found at this site. Somewhere out there was another maddened creature like herself. Somehow she had to find her.

She wouldn't find her though, the woman she sought was far away, hunting.

WHILE A FRIGHTENED and injured woman sought her former colleague, far away a wolf raced through an open field, zig-zagging as he fled. Above, a hunting hawk marked his path and the pattern of his evasive maneuvers. Suddenly, she folded her wings and stooped.

The hawk plummeted towards the ground, unfurling her wings at the last moment, and reaching for the wolf with her talons. She managed to touch his tail, but no more. She spiraled back into the clear blue sky as the wolf turned and ran back across the field.

He changed his pattern as he fled, but she marked him and again fell from the sky. Just as her talons reached for him the wolf turned in mid stride, reaching for her with powerful jaws. The hawk banked, turning in mid-air, causing the wolf to miss. Her wing gave him a buffet on the head as she climbed to high for him to reach.

The wolf stood watching as she returned to the air, lying lazily on an updraft high overhead. With lightning speed, he turned and raced toward the farmhouse in the distance and the barn just beyond. There was no evasion this time, just unbelievable speed.

A few beats of her wings and the hawk was ahead of him, diving toward the barn door below. As the hawk reached the ground she morphed into a naked woman. Her laugh of victory turned to a shriek as the wolf leaped at her. She ducked low and he transformed into a young man as his body passed above her. A forward roll brought him back to his feet in time for a bathrobe to settle over his head.

"Put your robe on before you scare Bill's chickens." The woman was grinning at him, and he was besotted all over again.

Shyly, he tied the robe and turned away so she couldn't see him blush. "That was fun, sweet Ronni. A good workout, too."

"Yes, it was, Igor. Yes, it was. We should probably be getting back now."

"Soon, my pretty bird. First, Igor has to catch his breath. You've worn me out. You've got me ruined."

She laughed at that and gave him a smile that fairly melted his young knees. "All right, let's see if Bill has any coffee brewing. Suddenly I'm hungry."

"Hungry? Why didn't you eat something? There were lots of mice in the field."

Laughing, she cuffed his shoulder then playfully poked him in the ribs to make him flinch. They reached the house to be invited in for coffee. "What's wrong, Bill? You seem a bit distracted."

Bill Walker was the Lair's lookout and resident farmer. "Oh, sorry, Ronni," he replied, as he passed her a mug of coffee. "It's that jersey cow, she's not doing too good. I was up half the night with her. Could you take a look for me?"

"Of course. Igor, would you be a sweetheart and go fetch my bag?"

"Anything for such a beautiful woman." He gulped down his coffee then stepped outside, morphed into the wolf, and raced away toward the mansion in the distance as the bathrobe settled to the ground. Fifteen minutes later a jeep stopped in the farmyard and the young man hopped out, her medical bag in hand. He tossed her a t-shirt and jeans, then followed the old man into the barn. Dr. Rhonda Stockman, also known as Lady Hawk, veterinarian, was close behind.

Much later that evening, a tired vet leaned against the young man's shoulder. "You okay, sweet Ronni?"

"Just tired, Igor. The cow will be fine now, but I need to sleep for a few days. How about you?"

"Da, I'm tired, but I like this."

"This?"

"Sitting under the stars with a beautiful woman leaning on my shoulder. Life is good to me."

She laughed at that. She berated herself for how much she loved being in this young werewolf's company. He was barely out of his teens, and she was nearing thirty. Still, she couldn't seem to help herself, nor did she really want to. "You won't think it so great if I start to snore."

"Stop now, you're spoiling my illusions. Sweet Ronni, I can feel the fatigue in your body. You need to eat then get some rest. Come, let us go back and raid Elaine's kitchen."

"Yeah, we should get back. So, wolf or walk?"

"Ride in style, beautiful lady. I stole Eric's jeep, remember? Come, court physician, your chariot awaits." He rose and offered his hand. She took it and let him help her to rise. Together they walked hand in hand back to the jeep.

TWO DAYS PASSED BEFORE the agent reported back to the director that he'd tracked down a phone number for the missing former agent. "You sure this is the right number, Egan?"

"Yes, sir. He's up north, working for some paranoid recluse on full retainer. Sir, you may have to reactivate him to get him to take on this one."

"Yeah, well, I'm not so sure I want to go there. I'll try bullshit first. Wish me luck."

"Good luck, and may God have mercy on us all if anyone ever finds out what Sawchuk was up to for the last couple of years before he quit." He sank into a chair as his boss dialed the phone.

SEVERAL PEOPLE SAT around a long table, chatting, and just enjoying the day. A powerfully built man furrowed his brow as he looked at his ringing phone. "Director Compton, what the hell does he want? Sire?"

The vampire king nodded his head and Terry Sawchuk answered his phone on speaker. "Director Compton, what can I do for you today?"

"To start with, Sawchuk, you can take me off speaker."

"No can do. Got my hands in muck. We're alone, you can speak freely."

"We'd better be. Look, Sawchuk, I'll get right to the point. We've got a case that's right up your alley. Totally weird shit, lots of blood and gore. Just the way you like it."

"And your own people are completely lost. You need this kept under the radar. Sorry, but I'm on retainer full time. Can't do it."

Suddenly the queen leaned over and whispered softly in Terry's ear. He nodded as the man on the phone went on. "Look, I don't give two shits about your retainer. If I have to, I'll reactivate you and ..."

"Oh, cut the bullshit," said Terry. "You're desperate, I get that. Your people can't, or won't, deal with it. Fine, I'll have a look.

"Here's how this'll work. I'll come look it over, and if I'm interested you'll provide me with a badge for myself and each of my team, as well as full access to all information concerning the case. If I take the case, I work independently and make the whole thing go away, no actual files turned in, no expenses turned in, and no actual reports turned in. Our fee is half a million. Two hundred fifty thousand up front and the rest when it's done."

"Jesus Christ, I can't justify that kind of expenditure without ..."

"Relax, we'll provide you with a plausible story to tell congress, give you a paper report they'll believe, and supporting docs to go with it."

"And not a goddamned word of it will be the truth."

"Forgive me, Director Compton, but if you wanted the truth you wouldn't have come to me in the first place, and we both know that. Oh, I'll need a fully equipped mobile lab."

"All right, Sawchuk, but don't screw this up. You're going to Boone, North Carolina, someone will meet you and your team there."

"So, has Egan Bridger been there?"

"Yes, the deputy director has been there, he'll meet you at the site. I'll e-mail you all the pertinent information."

"He's got to be in the room with you. Egan, what the hell am I looking at here?"

"Dammed if I know, Terry. It's ugly, messy, and right out of a bad horror movie. Philadelphia Experiment type of shit, only worse. Only bring team members with strong stomachs."

"Understood. See you there." He broke the connection then sighed. "All right, Sally, why did you want me to take this thing on?"

"Terry, I have a feeling this is something we should be looking into, not the government."

"You're thinking non-humans?"

"I'm getting a sense of that, yes." Queen Sally's psychic abilities had grown stronger over the past two years. These days her people acted on her hunches as though they were solid fact.

"Okay then, guess I should pick a team and hit the road. Sire?"

"Take whoever you need, Terry."

"Well. Since I have no idea what the heck I'll be facing, I'd like to wait until I get the information. I ..." His phone buzzed again. "Ah, here we go now. Tommy, want to pop this up onto the big screen so we can get a good look at it?" He tossed the phone to his friend who caught it easily. A moment later the big screen came alive with the photos taken by those who had discovered the accident.

"Wow, holy crap," mutter Terry. "Clara, can you make any sense of that?" The small woman rose and stepped closer to the screen.

"Oh my God," gasped another woman at the table.

"Ronni, what is it?" asked the queen.

"My queen, that's the lab I worked out of. I know that woman right there. Oh dear gods..." She was suddenly wrapped up in the queen's arms. Sally cooed soothing sounds for a moment then the woman relaxed. "I'm okay, I am. Thanks, Sally."

Clara Bynes, the resident crime scene investigator, and inventor, scanned the pictures carefully. "Ronni, how many people worked there?"

"At least ten, could be up to twenty on a given day, why, Clara?"

"Because I see evidence of only four here," she replied. "Five at most."

"Any idea what happened to them?" asked King Harald.

"I think I might," Clara replied. "Sire, when Ronni came to us, she spoke of what happened to change her. Ronni, that green dust we see here, is that like what you saw at the time of the change?"

"Could be, that's for sure. Why?"

"Because I think the people who investigated your disappearance took as much as they could of that dust to the lab. That would be a natural if they couldn't readily identify it. I think they took it back and, although it lay dormant for months, something triggered it. See here, there's body parts of lab animals fused to humans, rats, dogs, raccoons, etc.

"For some reason the changes didn't complete. They must have freaked out and tore each other apart. Now, in this picture, the lab door is wide open, that tells me several people escaped."

"Clara, what are you saying?"

"Sire, we could easily have a half dozen changlings, or people caught partway through a change, running loose in that area, maybe more. There could also be people who've turned into mindless creatures made up of several animals. I'd like to be on your team, Terry. I might be able to learn more from that lab."

"I want to go too," said Ronni. "I know a lot of those folks, and I know the area somewhat."

"I should go," said young Igor, as he stood up and looked from Ronni and then to King Harald and back again to Ronni. "You'll need someone who can track them through the forest, yes?"

Ella West, the group's matriarch and eldest of the vampires rose to speak. "I think perhaps that's a job for me."

Ronni's face had begun to redden as Igor gazed at her. She was grateful his attention had been diverted. Silently she fought the attraction to him.

"No, no, Great Mother," grinned the young man. "These people are already frightened. The saber-toothed tiger will just make that worse. A wolf is a more familiar animal and won't frighten them so badly."

"He's got you there, Mother," grinned the king.

The young fellow gulped as the tall elegant woman reached out to grasp his shoulder tightly. "Igor, I'll concede the point to you, but you must listen to me now. We've fought shoulder to shoulder before, and I hope we can do that again one day. I want your solemn promise you'll be extremely careful. No one but the team must ever see you change."

"I understand, Great Mother. The mission is not a place for play. I'll be careful."

"And obey Terry instantly, he'll be the alpha on this mission. Do you understand?"

"Yes, ma'am, I understand."

She didn't like it, but she relented and patted his shoulder then sat back in her chair.

"Who else will you need, Terry?" asked the king.

"I'll need Kylie's urban tracking skills in case some of these folks are hiding out in the cities, and maybe Clyde in case we have to have to talk one down first, or need a profile to work with. Now, here's the big one. Sire, what's the objective here?"

All eyes turned to the king as he sighed and gave that some serious thought. "In a perfect world, you would locate and bring all non-humans here; however, we rarely get a perfect world. Your call, Terry. If you can't bring some of them, or if you judge them to be too dangerous, do what you must. Just make certain no evidence of a non-human can be found."

"Understood, sire."

"You'll need a vampire on your team too," grinned Gudrun, Terry's wife. "Someone who can use the compulsion would be handy, don't you think? Ronni can't do it, neither can Igor."

"You're absolutely right, my love," replied Terry, as he smiled warmly at her, his eyes twinkling with mischief. "Do you think your buddy Marlene might have a few days to spare?"

Gudrun laughed at his teasing. "You'll never tear her away from her girlfriend, Lilly, for that long. However, I think I can make room in my schedule."

"Then my life is blessed," he grinned.

"Terry, take the plane."

"Yes, Sire, can I keep Eric with us as well? The man's got mad skills." The king nodded. "All right team, gather what you'll need. We'll leave first thing tomorrow."

Don't miss out!

Visit the website below and you can sign up to receive emails whenever Prudence MacLeod publishes a new book. There's no charge and no obligation.

https://books2read.com/r/B-A-ZKBBB-CWEXC

BOOKS 2 READ

Connecting independent readers to independent writers.

Also by Prudence MacLeod

Children of the Goddess
Lady Blue
Fallen Angel
Lady Justice
Lady Shadow
Lady Seeker
Watcher and Warrior
Shadow Ascending

Children of the Wild
Immortal Tigress
Children of the Wolf
Vampire's Lair

Forgotten Worlds
Suvi
Echo of the Past
Survivors
Ship
Fleet

Unite
IGEN
T.E.N.

Nova series
Novan Witch
Assassin of Nova
Beyond Nova
Claimstake
Red Nova

Watch for more at https://www.prudencemacleod.com/.

Telling a story is like knitting a sweater. Start with a ball of possibilities, pull out one small thread and begin. With luck and patience you will create something quite wonderful.

About the Author

On a far off windswept island Jennifer Crandall sits with her dogs and cats creating fantastic stories for all to enjoy. She publishes as JL Crandall, Prudence MacLeod, and Jenni Leigh.

Read more at https://www.prudencemacleod.com/.

www.ingramcontent.com/pod-product-compliance
Lightning Source LLC
Chambersburg PA
CBHW020953180626
46814CB00003B/1072